SWEETHEART

ACKNOWLEDGEMENTS

Heartfelt thanks to: Jeremy Poynting and Hannah Bannister of Peepal Tree Press for all the hard work; Geert, D., and J. for their support and encouragement; Michele Nayman for her copy editing skills and riffs on the semicolon; Deirdre Lynn and Velma Pollard for their friendly advice; Sheena Cumberland and the late Terrence Cumberland for their generosity; Marlene, Andrea and Elaine for being there through thick and thin; Yvonne, for her sense of humour; and Paola Boi, Giulia Fabi, Elisabetta Nones, Giuseppe Sofo and Luciana Tufani for their comradeship and kindness – grazie mille.

The author is grateful to the Caribbean and American national weather archives for their information on hurricanes, and she extends apologies to the newspapers named in the story.

SWEETHEART

ALECIA MCKENZIE

PEEPAL TREE

First published in Great Britain in 2011, reprinted 2012
Peepal Tree Press Ltd
17 King's Avenue
Leeds LS6 1QS
England

ISBN13: 9781845231774

Supported by
ARTS COUNCIL
ENGLAND

FOR MY MOTHER

CHAPTER ONE

CHERYL

JamAir Flight 15

Cho, Dulci, why couldn't you have been buried like everybody else? And why half of the ashes in Negril and half in New York? I just know these customs people are going to think it's drugs I have in this bottle. The last time they stopped me it was because of you as well. Bring me some cerasee tea when you come to the gallery opening, you said, I need it to pep myself up because I'm not feeling too well these days at all. And although everybody warned me – "Don't be a fool, girl; those customs people will embarrass you" – I still travelled with the cerasee. It was a chance to make up, to purge both you and myself of the bile of friendship gone wrong. But, of course, those customs people took one look at me and said: Open your bags. And there was the cerasee tea, right next to the Bombay mangoes your mother begged me to take you, and the hot peppers Aunt Mavis insisted on sending as a gift. Before I knew what was happening, they brought in their drooling dogs and their interrogation people. I tried to explain. Look, I said, it's cerasee tea. You know, to wash you out, I mean, it's a purifier, a de-toxer. They looked at me, eyes like stone. It cleanses your blood, I told them, makes you have, ah, bowel movements. I'm taking it to my friend. She's not feeling well. Finally they called our embassy there in New York and someone came to verify that yes, it was cerasee tea and perfectly legal at home.

They let me go but kept the tea, the mangoes and the peppers, saying I wasn't allowed to bring in farm produce, didn't I know that? When I told you about my ordeal, you laughed and rolled me a fat spliff, the first I'd ever had in my life. You coughed almost non-stop as we smoked it, a deep racking sound that seemed to come from the bottom of your chest. I knew you needed to see a doctor, but you waved away my concern and questions.

I wonder what the customs people are going to make of this Red Stripe Beer bottle now? I really wish I had a nicer container but this morning, just before I left Kingston, the damn urn slipped out of my hands and crashed to the floor, right in the middle of Norman Manley International Airport. And I'd been holding it so carefully. When he saw my tears, a lanky guy dressed in a blue baseball cap and loud white basketball shoes, offered to run upstairs to the airport canteen and fetch an empty bottle. I nodded without speaking and, when he came back, he got down on his knees beside me and helped to pinch up the ashes; we got most of it into the beer bottle. If we hadn't, people would've tramped through your remains – at least this half of them.

Through it all, I could hear you laughing.

So now I am on the plane, with three-and-a-half hours to go before we land at JFK, and I don't know whether this is bad luck or good fortune, but the man who helped me earlier is sitting in the same row as I am. He has an aisle seat, I am at the window, and the seat between us is empty: thank goodness for the space. He has a sweet, low voice that contrasts with the youthful clothes. I look him over and he turns to smile at me. I now notice the thick gold chain around his neck, with the outsized cross at the end, and I try to keep my eyebrows from going up. You always used to say, Dulci, that I was wrong to judge people by how they looked, but that's because you yourself were partial to loads of gold jewellery. Wearing tons of cheap-looking cling-clang gives a certain impression, you have to admit. Still, for all I know, this guy could be a cardinal and not a dancehall star.

He wants to talk, the last thing I feel like doing.

"So, who died?" he asks, gesturing towards the beer bottle, which I have tucked into the seat pocket alongside the safety-precautions card and the *SkyWritings* magazine.

"A good friend of mine."

"Sorry to hear that."

I look through the plane window at nothing and hope he'll get the hint that I'd rather be left alone.

"What killed him, or her?"

"Her. Cancer."

"Oh, a lot of people getting that now. Must be something in our food."

"Yes."

He reaches for the in-flight magazine, flicks rapidly through it and puts it back. The action reminds me of you. "Reading gives me a headache," you used to say. And right up to the end, except when the pain became too vicious, you had the clear beautiful eyes of someone who'd never read a book all the way through.

I turn again to look at the man beside me and he turns at the same time. His eyes are such a deep brown, and soft. He smiles disarmingly, and I feel like crying again. What is wrong with me!

"My grandmother died from cancer last year," he says. "The sickness drew her down to nothing. Pure skin and bones at the end."

"Yes, that's what it does to you."

"She raised me when my mother went abroad to work. Used to give me some big licks when I didn't do what she wanted. I never ever think I would see her like that."

"I hope she didn't suffer too much," I say, feeling my chest tighten. Skin and bones, that's what you were, too, Dulci. As light as a child.

"In three months she was gone. I was in New York doing some business, but I dropped everything and went home. I was with her at the end, and that's something I'm glad for. What about your friend? She used to live in New York?"

"Yes. And I was there at the end, too. But it's not something I can say I'm happy about. Anyway, the funeral was in Kingston. She just made me promise before she died that I'd take some of the ashes back to Manhattan."

"Mind the customs people, though. They might think you have chemical or biological weapon. That's all they can think 'bout now."

I laugh out loud, and he laughs along.

"By the way, what's your name?" I ask him.

"Danny," he smiles, and the openness of his face makes me catch my breath. You would like him, Dulci. If you were here in the flesh, I'm sure you would invite him to your apartment the minute the plane begins its descent.

"Mine is Cheryl."

"You know, Cheryl," he says, with an infectious grin. "When I saw you in the airport, I said to myself: I hope I get to sit beside that beautiful lady. So now I can't believe me luck."

Oh good Lord, what next? I'm sure you would have played along with him, Dulci, but I'm not in the mood.

"Danny, that's so sweet. Listen, I have a bit of a headache, so I'm going to take a nap, okay?" I inhale deeply, recline my seat and turn my face to the sky, eyes closed, remembering.

You moved into our neighbourhood when you were thirteen, Dulci. Do you remember how I laughed when I heard your father calling you by your full name, "Dulcinea Gertrude Evers"?

"Is where you get that name from?" I asked. And you kissed your teeth and didn't answer. Always feisty, that was you. Never bothered to waste your time answering unpleasant questions. I eventually found out that your father had named you after some character in a book by some long-dead writer. And you didn't appreciate it. Years later, when you landed in New York, you quickly rechristened yourself "Cinea Verse" and signed all your work with this name. It was memorable, in a way Dulci wasn't.

Your father, though, couldn't understand why you weren't proud to be Dulcinea Gertrude Evers. "Too full of herself for her own good," I overheard him telling your mother once. "If she would pay more attention to her lessons, she'd do better." And your mother smiled in her vague, distant way.

Your father was always a funny man, Dulci; it's something everyone knew right from the moment he set foot in Meadowvale. The way he turned your three-bedroom house into a semi-mansion had the whole neighbourhood talking, and people from other streets would come over to Hibiscus Drive just to walk past your house and gawk at the turrets and balconies. Your father must have been a king in a previous life, but he still didn't like you acting the princess – which came so naturally to you.

He always wanted more from you, wanted you to like the books and the music he loved so much. Do you remember the songs he taught us to play on the piano – "Jamaica Farewell", "Yellow Bird" and "Brown Girl in the Ring"? I was a quick learner, but you weren't, and your father would shout at you when you got a note wrong, his harsh bark belying his slight form. Meanwhile, your mother made sure she stayed out of the way of this short, wiry man who couldn't tolerate stupidity, as he was so fond of saying.

Everybody in the neighbourhood agreed that if you had inherited your father's feistiness and pride, you'd also been blessed with your mother's good looks: the flawless honey-coloured skin, the wavy hair, the big almond-shaped eyes. Mrs. Evers was still beautiful after having you and your five brothers, and she probably could easily have ditched your father and got herself a man who respected her, that is, if her mind had been in the right place. But your mother wasn't all there, was she, Dulci? The elevator just didn't go all the way to the top, as my Aunt Mavis used to mutter from time to time.

"So, sweetheart," your mother would say to me, "I hear that your Granny lives in England?"

"Yes," I would answer. "She left when I was a baby."

"And does she like Canada?"

"She's in England."

"Oh, yes. England. Do you want some lemonade?"

"Yes, thank you, Mrs. Evers."

"Does your Granny come home from America sometimes?"

And the questioning would go on, a different country each time, and the lemonade forgotten. It irritated everyone, most of all your father.

"Shut up, woman," he would shout from somewhere in the house. "You too damn stupid." But your mother never seemed to mind. She just smiled, her big eyes vacant.

As she often forgot people's names, your mother called everyone "sweetheart", including you, but she said it in a special way for her "one and only" daughter. "Sweetheart, your friend is here to see you." "Sweetheart, don't stay at your friend's house too long. Her mother has things to do."

"My aunt," I corrected her, for the millionth time.

When your father discovered that I was a student at Omega Academy, he went personally to the headmistress, Sister Marie, to beg her to let you in as well. He thought that changing schools might improve your grades, and your attitude. Well, the teachers tried, but the only "A" you ever got was in Art, not only because you could draw things seen and unseen, but because, let's face it, Mr. Walcott liked you. You never really had a head or a yen for studying.

Throughout the years at Omega, your father always screamed when he saw your report card, and he would go on for days about how good my grades were, but you eventually learned to stop crying and ignore him. Besides, you were the prettiest girl in our class. Who needs good grades when you're beautiful? Mr. Evers must have been around long enough to know this, but he foolishly believed brightness was more important than beauty.

Even on Sports Day, when he should've been the proudest parent, he still managed to be disappointed. "Well, she can run, but can she add two plus two?" was all he would say when you came first or second on the track. By then you had started referring to your father as "The Fool".

"Who cares what The Fool thinks?" you would shrug, after another put-down.

At Omega, you also played ping-pong and netball, and everybody wanted you on their team. You made it all look so easy, never seemed to sweat. Before we became friends, I'd never liked sports because I only had to get on the netball court for people to collapse in laughter at my clumsiness. "Just ignore them and enjoy yourself" was your advice. It's a lesson I still haven't learned fully.

I always envied your ability to take it easy, Dulci, to let gossip and bad luck run off you like rain off a banana leaf. When it came time for "O" levels, I swotted for nights in a row, while you said what will be will be, and went about your usual business – beach, movies and parties. I passed nine subjects, which ensured my place at university. You passed math, much to your surprise, and failed everything else, including art. You tried not to show it, but I knew that failing art must have upset you because it was the one thing you had felt sure of. A couple of months later, you started working at JamCom Bank and I headed off to UWI, but we saw each other on weekends. You came often to our student parties, and I would introduce you round. Not that you needed much introduction. Guys on campus were attracted to you like flies to curry-goat.

The air hostesses are serving food. Danny gently taps my shoulder and asks if I would like something to eat. I shake my head "no". I've stopped eating on planes because the turbulence always starts as soon as I take a bite of the mush. Danny tucks into the unidentifiable substance – the hostess said it was an omelette – on his rectangular piece of white plastic, and I admire his appetite.

He glances at me. "It not too bad," he says. "You should have some."

"I'm not hungry."

When he's done, he gazes at the beer bottle in the seat pocket. "I could do with a Red Stripe, but I guess it's too early for that."

I nod, thinking that I could do with something much stronger than a Red Stripe. A rum punch, for instance, with more rum than punch, even if I've never really liked the taste.

"Did your friend like beer?" he asks, looking again at the bottle.

"Yes. And lots of other things."

"She was how old?"

"Thirty-four."

"Wow! That's two years younger than me."

"Yes. She was ready to go, though, by the end."

I'll have to keep believing that, Dulci. That you were ready. You said you were, and even if you had changed your mind in the last moments, it was too late. You made me promise: whatever happens, don't back out. I had to keep the promise, right? I mean you had done so much for me, in so many ways. It was the least I could do.

I thought of all this during the funeral service, hoping that somehow I'd be forgiven. Seeing your father cry really got to me. And Aunt Mavis! I never knew she had tears. The woman put down one piece o' bawling. Everyone was shocked. Where did all that water come from in her dry, thin body?

But she always did like you, and her face used to break out into one of those rare smiles every time you walked through the gate and stepped onto our verandah. You'd been so curious about her when you moved into our neighbour-hood, this woman who hardly spoke.

"Your mother is really kind, but why she act so strange?" you asked.

I explained that Aunt Mavis wasn't my mother, although she looked like me. She was my mother's sister. My mother died before I turned two, and I don't remember anything about her. I knew her only from old discoloured Polaroid photographs. In one, she's standing in front of a picket fence and wearing a long wide-skirted floral dress, her hair pulled back in a bun. Tall and slim, she has a serious but touchingly sweet face. Aunt Mavis looked very much like her, except that the sweetness had long oozed out of her pores.

"And is Trev your brother or your cousin?" you in-quired. "The two of you could almost be twins." I didn't know how to answer, but I told you the story anyway, the first person I'd told it to, and you listened without com-ment.

After my mother died, Aunt Mavis and her son Trevor came to live with my father and me. Auntie never mentioned Trev's father, and Trev never asked about him, at least not when I was around. Trev was one year older than I, and we shared a room until I was about ten. Then my father added on a fourth bedroom so that each of us in the house could have our own room. Aunt Mavis was never still for a moment, she was always working – sweeping the floor, washing clothes, cooking. And she barely spoke to me, Trev or my father. She had eight words a day: yes, no, come eat, go to your bed. She never treated me any differently from Trev; we got equal-sized portions of tongue-burning food and the same responses to our questions.

Trev and I grew tough on Aunt Mavis' cooking. Everything was peppered and we had to learn how to eat it or go hungry because my father was a pepper-man and Aunt Mavis didn't see the need to prepare two separate pots. At dinner time, Trev and I ate with tears streaming down our faces and loud sniffles as the pepper took its toll. Daddy fed us huge amounts of Buckingham ice cream after each meal. Later we learned to eat freshly cut hot peppers without a single grimace and, when we made new friends, our favourite trick was to see how much pepper they could eat without running home bawling. (You passed the test with flying colours, Dulci.)

Aunt Mavis lived in a cloud we couldn't penetrate, and my father, while he spoiled us with toys and treats, was also distant. He worked such long hours as an accountant at Mutual Building Society that we were lucky if we saw him two hours daily during the week. Aunt Mavis called my father "Mr. Francis" to his face and "That Man" behind his back, and he called her "Miss Mavis". Every weekend he gave her housekeeping money in a small brown envelope with her name written on it.

We knew that my father had women friends because he went out every Saturday night and some nights he didn't come home until the morning. But we never heard anything about the women until he started seeing a barrister named Gloria Armstrong who had built a humongous house up on Jack's Hill, with money she had borrowed from Mutual. People who knew of the house always talked about the Roman columns. And there were whispers everywhere that my father was going to marry this rich woman, whose cousin was the Minister of National Security or something like that.

Gloria Armstrong was famous for making criminals walk free. That's what people said. "If you kill somebody, just go see Gloria Armstrong. She'll get you off scotch-free."

One Friday evening, my father announced calmly that we would have a special guest to dinner on Sunday, his friend Gloria, whom Trev and I were to call "Auntie Gloria". He asked Aunt Mavis to hold back the pepper because Auntie Gloria didn't like hot food. Aunt Mavis said sourly, "Yes, sah. Is you paying for it, sah."

On Sunday morning, my father plaited my hair himself. I never knew he could plait hair. It was strange feeling his big hands turning the strands of hair and tying in a ribbon. He was gentle, unlike Aunt Mavis. Then he told me to put on my prettiest dress. I choose a blue-and-white striped outfit that Aunt Mavis had bought me, and Trev put on black pants and a white shirt. Aunt Mavis kept on her house dress, an unbecoming grey bag.

Gloria Armstrong arrived at 12:30, in her shiny green Volvo. She was a tall, bony, light-skinned woman with bobbed black hair, but she had a kind face and laughed a lot when we were introduced. Every time she laughed we stared at her teeth – they would have made a rabbit proud. "You ever see buck teeth like that?" Trev whispered to me. I shook my head, mute.

Auntie Gloria had brought us presents: for me a white doll that could close its blue eyes, and a cowboy hat for Trev. I hadn't played with dolls in years, and I couldn't see Trev wearing that hat; he would have been laughed out of the neighbourhood. We said, "Thank you very much, Auntie Gloria."

The lunch was rice and peas, chicken with fried plantains, and a lettuce and tomato salad. It had no taste. Aunt

Mavis had not only held back the pepper, but also the salt, thyme, garlic and onions. While Daddy, Auntie Gloria, Trev and I ate in the dining room, Aunt Mavis sat outside on the verandah, talking to herself.

"Lord, it look like it goin' rain and I have so much clothes to hang out. What I goin' do wid dem, eh?"

Inside, Trev and I tried to eat the food but could manage only a few forkfuls. My father and Auntie Gloria ate heartily and, when the lunch was done, they told us they were going to take us for a ride to Hellshire Beach, although we wouldn't be able to swim since we had just eaten. Trev and I changed into shorts and tee-shirts and excitedly piled into Auntie Gloria's Volvo, waving to Aunt Mavis who kept her eyes on the ground and didn't wave back.

At Hellshire, Daddy told us the news. He and Gloria were planning to get married, but she wasn't going to come and live with us; he and I were going to live at her house.

"And Trev and Aunt Mavis?" I asked, while Trev hung his head, his chin seemingly glued to his chest. Daddy said I could visit them on weekends but that they would stay in Meadowvale because things were more "convenient" that way. I flew into a childish rage and said I wasn't going anywhere if Trev and Aunt Mavis couldn't come too. My father's face tightened and, for a brief moment, I thought he would hit me, but then Auntie Gloria laughed and said, "Let the child do what she wants, Francis. Children know their own minds these days."

Daddy stared at me, then at Trev, and I swear I'd never seen such a look of dislike on anyone's face. Trev didn't meet his gaze, and my father finally turned his eyes to the sea.

"Millstone round me neck," he said to no one.

When we got back home, the verandah was covered with broken plates, and Aunt Mavis was nowhere to be seen. We found her at the back of the house, in the laundry room, scrubbing the clothes as if she were trying to get out banana stains.

Wordlessly, my father cleaned up the mess on the verandah before leaving with Gloria. He told Trev and me he would be back the following night.

Within two months, my father had moved into the mansion on Jack's Hill, and I stayed on with Aunt Mavis and Trev.

When I'd finished telling you the story, Dulci, you said: "Well, I'm glad you living here in Meadowvale and not on Jack's Hill. But next time you go to visit you father and Gloria Armstrong, can I come? That house sound like something else."

I said: "Of course, no problem. You can come with me any time, as long as you give me one of your puppies." Your father had bought a trio of mixed-breed dogs to protect his castle, and one of them had just had puppies. You laughed and promised to see what you could do.

A few days later, you brought me my first pet. He had fluffy beige hair and light brown eyes, and he constantly wanted to play. Both Trev and I fell in love with him right away. We named him "Pepper" and were surprised at how much Aunt Mavis took to him. She made sure he always had food and water, and she even went to the pharmacy to stock up on de-worming medicine. Pepper rapidly became the most important part of the family.

As Pepper grew bigger, Aunt Mavis got into the habit of carrying on long monologues with him.

"But, Pepper, what I goin' cook this evening, eh? What you think 'bout ackee and salt fish with green bananas and some fry-plantains? That no sound good?"

And when Trev said, "That sound good, Mama" she ignored him. We hung around Pepper to find out what we would have for dinner, which people Aunt Mavis couldn't stand, and what my father had been up to.

"But Pepper, you see how man fool-fool? That woman must be telling him not to come look for his pickney. Is weeks now him don't show up. Not that we miss him at all."

You know, Dulci, I think Pepper saved Aunt Mavis' sanity. Maybe that's why she cried so much at your funeral. But, as I said, she always liked you. When your father threw your things outside and told you not to come back, I overheard Aunt Mavis cursing him to Pepper. "That damn man, treating his only daughter like that. Everybody makes mistakes."

But not every mistake gets into *The Star*, eh, Dulci. That, too, you could laugh about. Later.

Now that I think about it, Dulci, I guess you must have been lonely at home with five brothers, a not-quite-there mother and a father you could never be smart enough for. I was beside you when you showed him your final exam results. He took one look at the paper and said, "Get away from me, you dunce-bat." You bit your lips, and then smiled, as your father turned his back. You were right. The man was a fool.

His problem was that his children weren't doing the things he would've done if he'd had the chance. He'd wanted to become a teacher but hadn't been able to go to university because his parents couldn't afford to waste money that way. He'd gone into the building business by default, and used his brains to become manager of one of Babalon's construction companies, but his heart wasn't in it. He loved books and music and wanted to pass this on to his children, but your brothers only liked football and fights, and your dream was to be an artist. Your father always laughed when you mentioned art.

"Drawing and painting is something you do in your spare time," he told you. "Only damn fools try to make a living from that."

You tried to compromise by working at the bank when

we finished high school, but we both knew you should've been at the School of Art. You managed to paint a few pieces in your first months at the bank, but after you came to live with me on campus – illegally – you painted much more.

We had fun, didn't we, Dulci, despite having to hide it from the university that you were my long-term roommate and not just a frequent visitor? So the scandal had some positive results, even if you lost your job at the bank and had to leave home.

It wasn't your fault. The bank manager – Carlton Beckett – he should have known better than to start something with an eighteen-year-old girl. *We* didn't realize we were so young at the time! But *he* must have been in his forties at least, although he didn't look it. And he was a handsome man. Still handsome! My mouth almost fell open when he turned up at your funeral.

Did he give you the job because he fell for you during the interview? You did have that pass in math, so that was a plus, but it didn't take him long to come on to you. At first, you tried to keep him at bay, but soon you were tempted to go out with him, especially as he kept offering you rides home. The relief of not having to go home squashed in the rush hour buses and minivans made you appreciate good old Carlton more and more. Finally it happened: a weekend in Ocho Rios at Turtle Beach. Then a weekend in MoBay at Half Moon. And a full week in Negril at Hedonism. You told your father you were spending time with me, but you thought you were in love. Until Dakota struck.

Dakota Beckett, Carlton's wife, had been hearing all the news about the "young thing" that Carlton had taken up with. One Monday at midday, when the bank closed for lunch and you were making your way to Tastee's Patties on Harbour Street, Dakota accosted you at the bottom of the bank steps. She was a tall, tight-muscled woman, and she was dressed for war, wearing jeans, a man's shirt, and carrying a machete.

"You rass whore you," she screamed at you, and you told me later that you at first thought this was one of the many mad-people roaming the streets of Kingston. "You know who I am? I am Dakota Beckett and I goin' chop up you bumbo-claat for tiefin' me man."

After an initial freeze, you spun and raced up the bank steps, with Dakota in hot pursuit. Other bank tellers sprang out of your way and watched the drama wide-eyed. When you reached the top of the twenty-two steps and tried to push open the door of the bank, you found that it was locked and the guard wasn't looking your way. You beat on the door and the guard, recognizing you, made as if to open it, but at that moment, Carlton Beckett was just about to go out for lunch. When he saw what was taking place outside, he must have told the guard not to open the door if he wanted to keep his job.

You told me later that although you couldn't hear Carlton, you were sure that was what he'd said. As you continued to beat on the door, your eyes met his across the glass while Dakota grabbed your collar. Carlton swivelled and galloped across the bank lobby, back to his office.

"I goin' fix you rass business," Dakota yelled in your ear. You managed to grab the arm with the machete, and you twisted with all your might. The machete clattered down a couple of steps. But that didn't bother Dakota. She began to rip. First went your red linen jacket, part of the bank's uniform. Then fell the white cotton blouse – and your lacy black brassiere was suddenly on view for all. Dakota finally grabbed hold of the skirt, and you heard the sickening split before the torn linen dropped to the floor. As you stood there in bra, panties and high heels, Dakota rained blows on you. Not one of the watching tellers attempted to intervene. Finally, your humiliation became too much for the guard, and he opened the door, stepped outside and drew his gun. "Let her go or I going shoot you," he told Dakota.

"Shoot me, if you think you bad. Carlton goin' fire you rass claat." By then Dakota was holding you by the hair.

The guard fired a shot in the air to show that he wasn't joking, and the noise caused the spectators to scramble for cover. But Dakota held firm. The guard had to put the gun to her temple before she released you and you could flee inside the bank. The guard jumped in after you, slamming the door as Dakota retrieved her machete. She sat down in front of the bank and vowed to stay there until you came out, whenever that would be.

You ran to the toilet and stood there trembling until your friend Sandra, a teller at the bank, came down and took you to an empty office. She managed to get you a spare uniform, and she urged you to go and confront Carlton, who was no doubt hiding in his office. But you felt too ashamed. Sandra got you out through a back door and ran with you to Harbour Street to get a taxi. She had to give you money because your handbag was somewhere on the steps in front of the bank. The bank guard picked it up later, after Dakota had gone through it, taking everything of value.

The taxi brought you to the university. Luckily I was in my room when you arrived. I took you to the health centre, where they treated your bruises and cuts. Your face was swollen and would be like that for a couple of days, the nurse said. I phoned Carlton Beckett and told him that he was a first-class shit and that, although it wasn't any of my business, if I were you, I would hire someone to shoot him.

That evening he came to the dorm and begged you to forgive him. I made myself scarce, going to Trev's room for the night. You filled me in later. You said you had told Carlton goodbye, and that he'd taken it well. You said he told you he was still going to divorce his wife, and he promised not to fire the guard who had helped you.

The scandal made it to *The Star* the next day, with the headline: **Irate Wife Whips Bank Teller**. Your good fortune was that they got your name wrong, writing it "Dulcinea Rivers". Still it was enough for your father who had other channels of news about your behaviour. When you went home three days after the Dakota incident, your father had put all your things out on the sidewalk in front of his house. He told you never to set foot past his gate again, and all your mother's weeping and pleading were to no avail. But she managed to slip you several thousand dollars, and you came to live on campus with me. It was against the university's rules but lots of other students had permanent guests, so I wasn't worried.

As for Carlton Beckett, he lied: Dakota stayed with him, the guard went, and you were jobless for the next twenty-four months, except for your painting.

Not long after you moved in with me, you could laugh about the whole affair. "It's a good thing that my mother always taught me to wear nice panty and bra," you told me. You set up an easel in my room, brought in canvases and paint and said you were going to pursue what came naturally to you.

You weren't the only one doing what came naturally. Every time that you, Trev and I went to visit Aunt Mavis, we found she was getting weirder and weirder. She had set up some kind of business in the house. We lost count of the number of customers coming and going; they entered wearing frowns and left smiling, carrying away goods that Aunt Mavis had sold them, wrapped in plastic bags.

With Trev and I away at university and only old Pepper to take care of, Aunt Mavis had come into her own, selling "oil". Do you remember that, Dulci? Oil of *"bring me some money"*. Oil of *"make him stay home"*. Oil of *"make me have a pickney"*. Oil of *"make me no have no more pickney, me have enough already*". Aunt Mavis had gone into the oil business big time. Or had she always done it? I searched the past for clues.

"Remember Daddy got sick for months, after he moved out," I told Trev.

"Foolishness," he said dismissively. "Is all that pepper he used to eat that mess up his stomach."

"So how come we don't have no stomach problem?"

"Give it time. See if we don't have ulcer before we turn thirty."

"All right. But remember how soon after Daddy and Gloria got married she crash her Volvo and almost died?"

"The woman can't drive. You goin' blame that on me mother?"

"No," I said. "But how about the wedding cake? Is your mother made it, and everybody who ate it was shitting for weeks. Except for us because she did bake a special cake for us."

"I don't think Mama had anything to do with that. It could've been the curry goat that caused the shitting, and not the cake. And why you want to bring up that wedding anyway?" Trev said, getting vexed.

That wedding. How we laughed about it, afterwards, Dulci. It was the biggest fete Jack's Hill had ever hosted, and you finally got to see Gloria Armstrong's mansion. The nuptials took place a year after Daddy left, the time it took for Gloria to get divorced from her first husband. The living room of her fourteen-room mansion with the Roman columns was jammed with people on the wedding night, mostly Gloria's high-society friends, plus about twenty people from Meadowvale whom Daddy hadn't invited but whom Aunt Mavis had insisted should come along. You and your mother and father and your five brothers were there as well as several other neighbours.

Your father wandered around with awe – and envy? – on his face.

Gloria and my father had hired a band, and all night long the singer crooned such songs as "A Kiss to Build a Dream On", "I Can't Give You Anything But Love", and "Let's Stay Together". There was rum punch galore as well as wine and soft drinks. Curry goat as well as curry chicken. Rice-and-peas as well as plain rice. Salad combinations we'd never seen before. You, Trev and I ate so much our bellies bulged, and we explored the place, eavesdropping on everyone. We heard our neighbours wondering resentfully how Gloria had managed to get her hands on so much ackee and salt fish when everybody knew it was scarce. Then they remembered: Ah, but of course, she has a cousin who is a government minister. Ministers always know how to get salt fish.

And the cake, what a marvel: five layers of it. In a rare show of sweetness and forgiveness, Aunt Mavis had offered to make the cake. In fact, she had made two cakes, one for the big people, and one – with blue and yellow icing – for the children. The first cake towered white and glorious above the newlyweds as they cut it, and the guests oohed and aahed. But at least one person was not impressed with the show. I overheard your father saying to your mother, "Imagine spending all that money on food when the only thing people goin' to do is eat it up, belch and go home. Damn fools."

"On behalf of my wife and myself," began Daddy, as tradition demanded, "I would like to…" The rest of the sentence was drowned by a loud belch from Aunt Mavis. Gloria's friends stared at her, as she rubbed her chest.

Each time my father tried to give his speech, Aunt Mavis belched, more and more loudly. Finally, Daddy gave up and said, "Okay, everybody. Let's eat the cake." Aunt Mavis belched one last time, and got up and left before the cake was served.

It wasn't long afterwards that the mansion's seven bathrooms started getting a steady stream of visitors. The only people who didn't have running-belly were us children, your father (who watched his sugar intake and so hadn't had cake), and the band, who hadn't been offered any. Soon a stench floated out of the bathrooms and into the living room, forcing people out onto the verandah and into the garden. But those who went outside had to run back inside as their bellies betrayed them.

Even if Aunt Mavis hadn't been dabbling in the oil business back then, there still had been something strange about that wedding, right, Dulci?

I said to Trev: "Mind you, I not convinced she didn't put something in the cake. Still that was six years ago. I don't see any reason for her to start up this business now. And all these fool-fool people coming here and buying this stuff."

"Maybe it helping them," he retorted. "Listen, she is a big woman. She can do what she want."

"And another thing, selling *oil-of-make-him-love-me-more* is illegal in this country. You know that?"

I had just discovered this at university. Some scholar had come to give a speech entitled "The Paradigms of the Occult" and had told us that obeah was against the law according to our own constitution. The English had written this down way back when, so that they would have an excuse to hang any slave doing something they didn't understand. Aunt Mavis could get into trouble if she didn't watch out. All it needed was for some malicious neighbour to point a finger, although the chances of that happening were slim, for fear of the consequences.

"Jesus, I hope nobody I know at university hear 'bout this," I moaned to you, but you just laughed.

Each weekend, we came home to the house reeking of

Aunt Mavis's concoctions, which all had castor oil, pepper and chicken blood as the base. We discovered that privately Aunt Mavis disdained the chicken blood, but her customers swore by it. If chicken blood was part of the mixture, their faith increased. After Aunt Mavis had cut up, stirred and simmered things on the stove, she filled old jam jars with the product and labelled them neatly.

By the time we were into our second year at university, she was heavily into "Bible and key". People would come to her, crying that something of theirs had been stolen and wanting to find out the culprit. After listening, as usual without saying a word, Aunt Mavis would open the Bible to Psalms, put the big iron key from the washroom on the page, recite some gibberish and then start calling out people's names. The key would spin and fall off the Bible when the thief's name was spoken. We saw it happen once, and it scared us sleepless.

But you, Dulci, went beyond the call of duty in praising Aunt Mavis' "new venture", and how she lapped up your words! Just as you had impressed her when you ate Scotch Bonnet peppers without any sign of discomfort, now you pleased her no end by telling her you needed her help.

Someone from the Jamdung School of Art who had seen your work had invited you to take part in a group exhibition in New York, and you were ecstatic but also nervous. Aunt Mavis told you not to worry, she had a special oil for you. I was there to witness the anointment. First you had to take a bath in our house, and then you had to stand there naked while Aunt Mavis rubbed you from head to toe with some malodorous lotion she had made.

Why did you allow it, Dulci? Was it just to make her feel useful or did you really believe in her powers? Were you thinking of your father just up the road and what he would have said?

Perhaps I should have got anointed as well, because it

certainly seemed to work for you. Once you hit New York, there was no looking back. Cinea Verse was born: Caribbean artist without peer.

"Maybe you should let me carry the beer bottle for you." Danny's voice jerks me back to the present on the JamAir flight.

"What?"

"I don't think they goin' let you through with it."

We both stare at the bottle.

"They will probably be quicker to stop you than me," I tell him. "I'll try to hide it in my carry-on bag once we land."

"They're searching everybody nowadays. When I was coming home, they stopped this old woman and made her take off her church-hat and even her shoes."

"Well, if they find the bottle in my bag, I'll just have to explain that my friend wanted to spend more time in America, where she had some of the best days of her life."

"Doing what?" Danny asks.

"I bet you're a lawyer, you ask so many questions," I laugh.

But he shakes his head. "I sell auto parts. It's the best business you can have on the island – after drugs, guns and rum bars. Every day hundreds of cars getting mashed up because of potholes or bad-driving. And then people run to me."

"Well, no wonder you can afford to wear gold chain," I tease.

He looks surprised. "Oh, this was a present from my grandmother. I been wearing it since she died."

What would you have said, Dulci? I'm so embarrassed that I can barely utter "Excuse me, I need to go to the bathroom."

I squeeze past him and make my way gingerly up the aisle, waiting for the usual turbulence to strike. It never fails once you start eating or heading for the toilet.

This time I'm lucky, but when I come out of the cubicle, I find the aisle blocked by the stewardesses and their trolley, so I stand there looking at the passengers facing me. The variety of hairstyles is astounding: braids, dreadlocks, creamed straight hair, plaited hair, jeri-curls, bright red wigs. And then there's the headgear – straw hats, woollen tams, baseball caps (turned every which way), scarves, turbans. They might have come from one of your paintings, Dulci.

"She was an artist. You never heard of her, Cinea Verse?" I ask Danny, when I'm back in my seat.

"The name sounds familiar," he replies, but his eyes are blank.

He must be one of the few people who haven't heard of you, Dulci, because within months of your first show in New York, you were everybody's darling. Nobody at home could understand it, and I heard people saying: "Only in America". You had found not only your calling but your destiny. I knew you'd never come back if you could help it. And it was so easy to stay on, wasn't it? Before your visa ran out, you got Josh to marry you. I stayed with you both when I came to visit, and it made me cringe to see how he worshipped the ground you walked on.

Josh – short, slim and balding, but not bad for middle-aged – taught art at NYU and was well-connected. When he took us out to dinner at a new "in" restaurant on Broadway, it seemed that all the diners and waiters knew him, and couldn't wait to get to know you. He provided you with a ready and willing market for your work, bought you expensive art books, which you never read, and got his friends at *The Times* to write about your shows.

When you left him a few months after you'd received your green card, he quit his job and moved to Florida, taking a dozen of your paintings with him.

"I let him have them," you told me, with a carefree shrug. "It was the least I could do." You insisted that your leaving him had nothing to do with getting your green card, it was just to escape the "terrorism of the know-it-all". It was true: Josh did talk too much and too loudly, especially about art, and he was always deeply wounded when you showed not the slightest interest in his famous-artist stories. Still, although it really was none of my business, I stopped speaking to you for a while because I thought Josh had deserved better

But who could stay angry with you, Dulci (I mean, except for your father)? Even I eventually had to agree that if Josh wanted to marry a woman half his age, then he had to take the consequences. Besides, I loved visiting you in New York and soaking in the glamour of your art openings, where it seemed everybody called you "sweetheart" or "darling" and wanted to be your friend.

At one opening, a woman wearing blue eye-shadow, orange face powder and a tight, beaded dress she should have given to her granddaughter, sidled up to me and whispered enthusiastically, "Cinea looks so much like Chayonce, don't you think?" I watched you, flashing your hair, sticking out your chest and smiling distantly at your admirers, and all I could do was nod.

I came to see you nearly every school holiday, glad to get away from home and also from the hooligans in the classroom. You always said you didn't know why I went into teaching when there were so many other things to do. "Try something else," you advised. "Stop wasting your time." But to live like you, Dulci, you need talent and looks. I could add two plus two every time, but I didn't have the imagination to get anything but four. Not to mention the looks. My face is okay, as Trev used to say, but my nose gets in the way.

Each time I came to see you, Dulci, you were thinner,

more beautiful, and had a different man living with you. I lost track of the names, except for smiling, curly-haired Ricardo, who said "Let's have some fun", seconds after you left us alone in the apartment one day.

"Fun?" I asked, not quite sure what he meant.

"Yes, let's go into the bedroom and fool around."

I had to laugh, and he chuckled, too, without the slightest embarrassment.

"Cinea wouldn't mind," he declared. "In fact, why don't you join us in bed tonight?"

I laughed again, this time really loudly, and his amused shrug said: "Nothing tried, nothing gained".

It was only after you told him to move on, Dulci, that I related the incident. "You could have slept with us if you wanted," you responded. I thought that you were joking, or that New York had corrupted you. Confused, I decided to stay away for a while, but you kept asking me to come back.

When I did, I was shocked at how thin you had become, and I thought you had succumbed to anorexia.

"You need to eat more," I told you. "Get some Big Macs and milkshakes."

"Bring me some cerasee tea next time you come," was all you said. And you repeated the request several times before I left, as if to make sure I wouldn't forget.

But Customs seized the cerasee tea, and I ended up forcing you to see a doctor the day after I arrived in New York, the day after they opened the gallery with your name on it. How much weight had you lost by then? How long had you been smiling through the pain – just like you did when we fed you freshly cut peppers all those years before?

When all the tests revealed the truth, you made me promise not to tell anyone until you were gone. That was only the small promise.

A month later, when you had turned over your paintings

and sketches to the gallery, and when the apartment had been sold and you were ready, you called me back to New York to fulfil my pledge of going to hell with you.

That's what it was, Dulci. Hell. Being forced to watch you starve yourself. "Even if I beg you, don't call the doctor, don't give me any food, just let me go. I don't want to hang on for months like this or have anyone cutting into me."

Why did I agree, and why did you need me there in the first place? We spent our time saying things that would have been better left unsaid. But that was one of the ways to shorten the hours – talk. We talked while you sketched, and our words hung in the apartment, framing your drawings. For the first three days, I sat, lay, stood in an array of poses, and you filled page after page, until the weakness claimed you. I'd never posed for you before, not even when we lived together. In the evenings, you chased me out to feed myself, while you continued your fast. And although I never managed more than a few forkfuls, even those filled me with the deepest guilt, Dulci.

On the fourth day, after we each knew everything, I reached my breaking point.

"Why do you have to do this?" I screamed. "There is medicine. There is surgery. Let me call the doctor."

But you only smiled. "Cheryl, I'm ready to go. I really am. And this way, I feel whole. Come on, stop the crying."

Later, you urged me to go to a hotel. "Don't stay. It will be all right." But I couldn't leave, and so you came up with the pretext of sending me to the gallery with the last drawings you had done. Suspicious, I still went and, when I came back, you had locked me out. I broke my promise then and called the police, and they finally forced the door open.

We found you lying on the sofa in the living room, your eyes closed, a smile on your face. I lifted you up, even as the police tried to stop me, and it was like holding a child.

Afterwards, I had to take you home for your funeral, and listen to your father weeping and wailing. That was the worst.

Now here I am on what will be my last trip to New York. I'll scatter the ashes in Riverside Park, where we went jogging so many times. That is, if I get through Customs.

Danny touches my shoulder. "Listen, sweetheart, don't worry," he says. "If they give you any trouble, I'll just rub the ashes on my arms and chest like talcum powder and then we can wash it off later wherever you like."

I want to answer but can't get the words out. What a brilliant idea.

I can hear you laughing your head off, Dulci.

CHAPTER TWO

DESMOND EVERS

Hibiscus Drive, Kingston

I always imagined the reverse happening: that you would be bent over my body, crying, full of regret that you hadn't been a better daughter. That's the way it should have been. Sometimes I think you went first just to spite me, just so I would have to see the anger and blame in your mother's eyes. Every day. *Every* minute of the day. She has your eyes. You had her eyes – those clear light brown pools that I can no longer look into.

I overheard someone gossiping about me the other day: "Yes, it hit Dulci's mother hard, but just imagine how the father must feel. He must feel worse than dog."

If you'd been there, Dulcinea, you would've queried right away: "How you know how dog feel?" That's the kind of feistiness you were born with. No one could tell you anything, least of all me. I didn't understand you. Children are supposed to listen to their parents, do what they tell them. But you could never listen to anyone, except for that madwoman Mavis, with her obeah foolishness. By rights you should have been her daughter. You got born into the wrong family.

From the moment I saw you in your mother's arms, I knew that you were going to be trouble. Babies shouldn't have such bold eyes. I felt you were staring me down, and it took me a while to get rid of the sensation.

"She can't even see you," your mother said. "She can only see fuzzy shapes and colours right now."

She probably learned that from one of the baby books I bought her, if she ever read any of them. The woman can barely get through the headlines in a newspaper. I don't think words make any sense to her. In forty years of marriage, I still don't know what goes on inside her head. Probably nothing. And her sons all take after her. You were different, you were bright, but stretching your mind was just too much work.

Still, with all the irritation you caused, I was proud of you. Proud of the way you carried yourself, proud of the way you never allowed anyone to put you down. I should've told you this, at least once, before things got out of control. I'll never get rid of the guilt for doing what I did, but I felt you had shamed me. I couldn't overlook all the lies you'd told about spending time with Cheryl when you were carrying on with that man. Did you have to lie to me, knowing how much I cannot abide lying? When you and the boys were growing up, it was the one thing that made me angry – the lying, and yet I never laid a hand on any of you, unlike my own father.

I learned not to lie or to do anything to provoke my father early on because Samuel Evers was a vicious human being. When you were little, you saw my back with the ridges of skin from badly healed wounds, and you asked me what had happened. I don't remember what I told you but you were not satisfied with the answer. You kept asking until I lost my temper. How could I tell you that your grandfather would beat his children so much and so often that we would be covered in welts for days on end?

He also had something special for me as I was the only boy. If he thought I had lied or stolen something, he would tie me to the mango tree in the front yard and then beat me with a cane, so all the neighbours could see. When my mother put Vaseline on the cuts later, she would beg me to forgive him. "It's the illiteracy," she would say. "That's why he can't control himself. He's just so frustrated."

Your grandfather couldn't read or write. Did you know that, Dulcinea? But every Sunday afternoon he would sit out on the verandah facing the street, with the *Gleaner* opened wide in front of his face, fooling no one. The neighbours swapped jokes about him holding the newspaper upside down without ever noticing. Mr. Duncan from up the road always had a comment when he passed our house and saw my father with the paper: "Sammy, what *is* the prime minister saying today?" Or: "Sammy, why are all the boats in the harbour upside down?"

When I grew too big and strong for Sammy to tie me up anymore, I got my revenge by reading aloud. Every Sunday as he sat there with his newspaper, I would take a book, go sit in the yard, and read the story at the top of my voice. My mother had the collected plays of Shakespeare in an old battered volume, and I read it aloud from cover to cover, while my father sat cowering behind the newspaper that was a mystery to him.

Samuel Evers. He was a man you never argued with because he was always right. No one could ever make him change his mind about anything. He had the stubbornness of the illiterate. Backing down on any topic would only show what a fool he was, and that he couldn't afford. So his voice would bellow through the house, and the cane would come out and whip through the air at the slightest sign of opposition. My two sisters and I escaped from him by reading our mother's books and playing her piano. And all the time we wondered why a schoolteacher had chosen to marry such a moron. None of us has ever laid a hand on our own children. You know that.

The only thing my father knew how to do was build. He built our house with his own hands, and he earned good money from fixing other people's homes all over the parish.

He taught me everything about construction – something I was certain that *I* would never end up doing. But I had no choice. My father refused to spend any of his hard-earned money to send my sisters or me to university. At the end of high school, we were on our own, our brains in limbo. I was lucky to get a job with the Babalons, building houses and hotels, and your aunts later became secretaries in the Ministry of Education.

When you were growing up, I took you to see some of the buildings I had worked on, buildings my father could never step foot into. You would look around in wonder, asking: "You built this, Daddy?" Your eyes would be wide with admiration. It made me feel like a king. I was never out of work, and the money I earned made your grandfather's income seem like peanuts.

I saved thousands of dollars to send you and your brothers to university, but not one of you worked hard enough to go. Your brothers only know how to play football and live off the fool-fool women who keep taking them in, and you, with all your brains, you just couldn't do enough to pass your subjects. If Cheryl got such good grades, why couldn't you? And Cheryl's father wasn't even around most of the time. All she had was that madwoman talking to herself or to that damn dog who, by the way, has been replaced by three mongrels. Three mangy half-breeds.

I tried to teach you so much, Dulcinea. Yet Cheryl is the one who went to university and became a school teacher, and that boy, her cousin or whatever – he's now a doctor. Imagine that. And both of them are still living here in the neighbourhood, sharing a house right next door to the madwoman and her dogs. You know, I always expected those children to run as far away from her as soon as they could, but I guess blood is thicker than water. Or maybe they stay here to keep an eye on her so that she doesn't get out of control.

Yes, you could draw, Dulcinea, but I didn't think art was going to do anything for you. Every fool on this island can draw coconut trees and blue sea in the background, and who is going to pay them for it? I wanted more for you.

"Boy, this child is so bright. She's going to go far, you know, Desmond." That's what your grandmother always said when we went to visit her. And your mother would sit there smiling like a Madonna – as if you'd inherited your brains from her.

By the time you were born, your grandmother was living in her own house, a place I'd built for her when she'd finally decided to leave Samuel Evers. You loved her house, with the wide verandah and the swings hanging from the grapefruit trees in the back. The land itself had been part of a farm, and my mother used the money she'd saved from her teacher's pension to buy it, while I paid for all the materials to build the house, choosing expensive green-and-white ceramic tiles for the floors, and the best wood for the louvre windows. I made the ceilings high so that the rooms would be cool. Maybe somewhere in the back of my mind, I was also building for a daughter, and for grandchildren.

I never took you to my father's house, and you never met him, although you would have if you'd come back from New York for your grandmother's funeral. Samuel Evers was there, his tears falling on the programme that he couldn't read. You sent a wreath, but you didn't come. And your mother blamed me for that empty space in the church. It was there in her eyes.

Five boys, then you. "You're a lucky, man," the doctor told me. "You finally have a daughter." Another mouth to feed, but one that would eat less. That's what I thought. For that first year, you were your mother's business, until you started walking. Then you always walked to me. You loved it when I lifted you up and threw you into the air. Your laughter would ring through the house, and you always wanted more. For so long, that was our favourite game. But your mother didn't like it – she always thought that one day I would drop you. It never happened.

When did things change? When did I become the enemy, the Fool? I know that's what you called me when you thought I couldn't hear you. Or perhaps you wanted me to hear. I look at my hands that built this house, making your room the most special, and I wonder how I lost you. Yes, I put your clothes outside, and told you to go, but it was only to teach you a lesson. I thought you would come back within a few days, repentant, asking for forgiveness. I thought we could try again. But the days turned into sixteen years, and you never returned. You walked right past my house to meet your mother at Mavis's place. And then you left for New York. Whenever you called, and I picked up the phone, you would only say, "Hello, may I speak to Mommy?" And I always said, "Yes, I'll pass you on". Why couldn't I have said "Talk to me this time. Just for a little bit."?

It's been two weeks now since your service, and this morning Cheryl came to tell me she was taking some of your ashes back to New York, as you'd requested. I wished she had told me earlier because I would have gone with her. But that's the trouble with young people nowadays. They never tell you anything until it is too late. I wished her a safe trip.

After she left, I tried to get ready to go to work but I didn't have the energy to get into my clothes, so when the postman rang his bicycle-bell, I went to the gate in my pyjamas. He handed me a long cardboard tube, flashing me that look of sympathy I hate. Everybody knows too much on this blasted island.

The tube was from you; it had your name written in full – Dulcinea Gertrude Evers – but no return address. Rolled tightly inside was a large piece of canvas. I carefully pulled it out and spread it open on the dining table. The surface was rough from your brush strokes, and the colours were so bright in the morning light. I stared at the painting of a thin brown man holding a little girl aloft in the air, both faces glowing with smiles. Your mother came to stand beside me to look at it for a minute. She glanced over at my wet face, my tears streaming down, then she walked through the door and out the gate, still in her nightie. I guess she was going down the road to Mavis' house. I don't know when the two of them became such good friends. Do you think those crazy women are plotting to poison me, Dulcinea?

CHAPTER THREE

CARLTON BECKETT

Kingston

"Look, your sweetheart dead."

That's how my wife broke the news to me, Dulci.

On a rainy morning she slapped *The Gleaner* down on the table as I was having breakfast and gave me a look that I can't even begin to describe. Scorn and hatred and resentment and pity. The woman has serious issues. I don't know why I'm still with her. But I'm too old to go anywhere else now.

Your picture was on the Obituaries page, which *The Gleaner* always puts in its "Entertainment" supplement. I'm going to write them a letter about that. It's like everything is entertainment in this country – death, violence, politics.

But there was also an article about you on the back page of the paper. A glowing item about how you put the island on the map in the international art world. The people at your gallery probably never told you this, but I made the bank buy one of your paintings three years ago. It hangs there in the lobby, to remind your colleagues that you rose above that little incident with my darling wife. We're all still at the bank, you know, doing the same old thing. I plan to work until I drop because retirement only means spending time under home-guard.

I'll always regret that I didn't come out to rescue you when Dakota attacked, but that would only have made things worse. Just imagine if she had chopped up both of us with her machete? She would have got off scot-free too, with an insanity plea. The woman is truly mad, believe me. Sometimes it seems like all the women on this island are mad, except for you. You were the sanest person I knew. But I had other reasons for not coming out on the bank steps. Maybe it was from revenge. You know what I'm talking about, don't you? Or didn't you realize that I saw you with the lifeguard?

Your picture in the newspaper was beautiful, just a head and shoulder shot, but I could see the rest of you, feel the rest of you. I've never had anyone else like you, Dulci. I could feel the blood coursing through my body just from looking at your picture. And the rain falling outside reminded me of that little trip we took up the Blue Mountains to Strawberry Hills. It was our first weekend away, and I kept my arm around your shoulders for the whole drive, steering round the bends with one hand. We admired the scenery – the deep green valleys and lush vegetation – and you smiled every time my fingers stroked your breast. It started raining just as we reached Strawberry Hills, and by the time they showed us to our wooden hut, it was pouring. We could do nothing but stay in bed and make love over and over again, as the rain pounded the zinc roof.

After that first weekend, I was like a man addicted to ganja or something even stronger. I couldn't get enough, and the more you gave the more I wanted. I wanted to marry you, but I knew deep down that you wouldn't have stayed with me. If Dakota hadn't gone on the rampage, how much longer would it have lasted? After three months you were already getting tired of me. I knew it. But by then I didn't have much pride left.

Did you ever tell your friend Cheryl the whole story, Dulci? She was so contemptuous when I came to see you at the university, so angry. Yet you took the whole thing as a joke almost. "Carlton, we both had fun, but I'm the one who got beaten. So let's just forget it." That's what you told me. I kissed your bruises, your cuts, the black and blue marks, and undressed you in Cheryl's dorm room. And even though you kissed me back and groaned my name, I wasn't at all fooled. It was the end.

"Your wife deserves you more," you said as you put your clothes back on. It was said with a smile, without sarcasm, and I had the strange impression that you were already far away, even though the room was only ten feet wide. That was something you were good at, Dulci – being there and being gone. Even at eighteen years old. In that moment, I felt ancient, at forty-seven.

How old was the lifeguard? He was what, twenty-five? The sonofabitch. We'd driven up to Ochie that Friday afternoon. You pretended to be sick, so that you could leave the bank early, and my secretary knew that I had a meeting with someone in the Ministry of Finance and that I would be off for the rest of the day.

I told Dakota that the bank was holding a weekend conference in Ocho Rios, and I don't know what you told your father, who probably would've built a prison for you if he could. That's what you always claimed, anyway. When we got to Turtle Beach Hotel we took an evening dip in the pool, then went for a walk along the private beach. Everything was perfect, the sunset, the sound of the sea – and then that guy came up to tell us not to go into the water because of jellyfish spotted that day.

He was one of those show-off types, it was obvious right away. Arm and leg muscles bulging every which way, and a tee-shirt without sleeves so everyone could see how much time he spent doing push-ups. And the tight vulgar swim trunks, as if he was the only one in the world who had something worth flashing.

"I'm the lifeguard here," he grinned at you. "Don't go swimming if I'm not around." He chuckled as if he'd just

44

told the greatest joke. Couldn't take his eyes off you. As we prepared to walk on, he commented: "It's nice to see a father and daughter on holiday."

I was just too stunned by his gall to do anything, but you were quick, as always. "He's not my father," you replied. "We sleep together." You walked off, with me trailing behind, feeling like a fool and having that annoying chuckle echo in my ears.

That night in our room you tried hard to make things work but my usual stamina had deserted me. I felt the years between us.

The hotel served breakfast by the pool, a dazzling array of watermelon slices, papaya, mango, fried plantain, roasted breadfruit, golden-brown dumplings, ackee and salt fish. I was looking forward to the feast, until I saw him. Strutting around the pool, pretending to be looking after the people swimming. Someone could have drowned and he wouldn't have noticed because his eyes kept following your every move. He watched you as you got up to get some juice – thoughtfully bringing me a glass too – and he watched you as you sat down. I watched him watching you, though you seemed oblivious to the charade.

You held my hand after breakfast as we sat there eyeing the swimmers (foreign tourists who couldn't get enough sun), and at one point you rested your head on my shoulder. You seemed quite content to sit there, even after the hotel staff cleared away all the breakfast things, but I'd had enough of the scene.

"Let's go for a walk on the beach," I said. You looked up at me with those clear, beguiling eyes and stretched your arms above your head, sticking out your breasts. "You go ahead," you instructed, with the sweetest smile. "I'm going to rest in the room some more." You rose from your chair, kissed me and sashayed back in the direction of our room.

I stood there hesitantly for a few seconds before walking

to the beach, feeling as if I was drowning. What could I do? I couldn't tie you up, or beg you to "behave", could I?

I came back in twenty minutes, and I knew what was happening even as I stood outside the door. I opened it quietly, and Mister Lifeguard was there, his muscled behind vigorously going up and down while your arms clung to his back. I spun round and went back to the beach, thankful for miles of white sand. When I returned you were sleeping, no doubt exhausted, and I lay beside you, sleepless, until dinnertime. We left early the next morning, speeding back to Kingston.

Did you tell Cheryl, about that? You once said there were no secrets between you, that you were closer than sisters. But I bet you didn't tell her everything. She thought I was the one who pursued you and then fled when Dakota went on the warpath. But it wasn't that way, was it, Dulci?

Still, I have to say that Cheryl was nice to me at your funeral. She looked at me with sympathy, as if something had changed. But she's older and probably wiser now, and she must know that you were no innocent little kid-goat. I wished I could have asked her what you told her, but it wasn't the right place or time.

You know, I had hesitated when I read where the service was being held, but I'm glad I went, after all. We never did say a proper goodbye, my sweetheart.

CHAPTER FOUR

DAKOTA BECKETT

Cherry Gardens, Kingston

I wanted to kill you, Dulcinea Evers, just to teach you a lesson. You couldn't go fooling with a married man without expecting something to happen. What was in it for you? Weren't there enough boys your own age around?

I know, of course, what was in it for Carlton: a young body to make him feel more powerful, to keep the years at bay. You weren't the first one, you see. No, in the forty years (next September) of marriage, I've lost count of the number of girls. Each month he pays out a good portion of his salary to at least three of them who have had children with him, children that I've never seen.

None of the girls were ever a threat, though. They came and went, he took care of the children when accidents happened, and everybody knew where everybody stood. Until you came along to mess with the order. For the first time Carlton mentioned divorce, and I thought: over my dead body. Or over yours, Dulcinea Evers.

I knew all about you from my friends at the bank: that your uniform was shorter than everybody else's and your heels higher; that you had a way of smiling and opening your eyes wide when you dealt with male customers; that your hair always looked as if you'd just come from the hairdresser; that you thought you were better than the other tellers because apparently bigger things awaited you.

Everybody knew about you and Carlton. You could at least have tried to hide it, but perhaps you wanted to flaunt your control. For the first time, Carlton wasn't the one calling the shots, the sad old fool. You caught him in his mid-life crisis – that's what my friend Pauline said. Her husband was not nearly as weak as Carlton, but in his late forties he also took up with a woman less than half his age, and began talking foolishness about leaving Pauline. She promptly poisoned him, and he spent days in the hospital recovering, thinking that God had sent him a sign to improve his ways. Pauline made sure she stayed at his bedside, praying the whole time.

But I couldn't do that to Carlton; I'm not a religious person and I don't know anything about poison. Pauline, you see, is a pharmacist.

The way Carlton carried on with you, though – all the lying and sneaking off to hotels on the north coast – filled my heart with a white-hot rage. I hated you. What did you know about commitment and being there through thick and thin? All these years I'd put up with Carlton's fooling around, swallowing the tears, because I knew that deep down he's a good man.

Carlton and I met when he was a student at the university studying finance and I was working in the library there on campus. His politeness was the first thing that struck me, when he came to ask if we had this or that book. And he was attractive, with his tall frame, square face and beautiful even teeth. When he looked at me and smiled, a warmth moved from my face to my feet.

He seemed to spend a lot of time in the library and, one afternoon, out of the blue, he invited me to go to Carib Theatre to see a show with him. It was *To Sir, with Love*, and we both loved it. Later, Carlton walked me home, holding my hand. He was twenty-two years old and I was twenty-six. Most of my friends were already married, but I didn't feel I was missing anything. With my light skin and long hair, I'd had my share of proposals, but I was picky. I wanted a quiet, secure life, like the one my parents had. They'd been married forever.

Carlton lived with his mother – his father had gone to England when he was about five – and I knew that money was tight, but he tried not to show it. He never let me pay for anything. We went to see many more shows after our first date, and he was always a perfect gentleman, in every way.

I was the one who took him to my house one evening when my mother and father were out. I was the one who took my clothes off first, to show him how much I loved him. And afterwards, I was the one who couldn't stop smiling.

When we discovered I was pregnant, Carlton said we should get married right away, although he still had a year to graduate. We had a lovely ceremony at the university chapel, with all our family and friends. I wore my mother's old wedding dress, white and lacy with beadwork that you couldn't find today, and Carlton wore a light blue suit that he'd borrowed from a friend. We were both happy about the baby. I began shopping for little things right after our weekend honeymoon in Port Maria.

But five months later I had to give birth prematurely after I fell off the stepladder in the library, while reaching up to replace a book. It was a boy, a tiny honey-coloured baby. He lived for twenty-five minutes. Have you ever known such pain, Dulcinea Evers? I cried for weeks, and nothing Carlton said or did could console me. When my grief subsided, I noticed the distance that had grown between us.

Still we tried once more, kept trying, but I never could conceive again. No one knew what had gone wrong. Meanwhile, some of Carlton's lady friends from university started whispering malicious things in his ear, that I had tricked him into marrying me by getting pregnant in the first place. That's how wicked people can be.

When Carlton got his first good job at the Bank of Nova Scotia, I left the library and devoted myself to taking care of him, watching him rise in his profession. He is a brilliant man, and there was no stopping him. He bought me this house in Cherry Gardens and made sure I never wanted for anything. And he was discreet about the women who flung themselves at him. A man in his position in a country like this will always have girls willing to do anything to get some extra pocket money. They probably all hoped he would leave me for them, but I never felt the slightest bit threatened. Until you came along.

What was it you had, Dulcinea Evers? Seeing Carlton in his fever of addiction, his willingness to throw away our life together, made me go a bit mad. I can honestly say that I don't remember going to the bank with that machete until I found myself there waiting for you. I just wanted you gone.

Later at home, I waited in tears for Carlton, who didn't show until late in the night, looking like a whipped puppy. I had expected fury, and was prepared for him to pack up right away and leave, but he said nothing. You had sent him back to me. The next morning at breakfast he quietly mentioned that divorce would probably be best, and I nodded agreement. But the following day, nothing was said, or the day after that. Both of us lay low and licked our wounds.

Out of respect for Carlton, the editor had withheld my name in *The Star* but the story was too juicy to kill. They needed to sell copies, after all. Your name was there, misspelled, and I felt everyone knew who the "bank manager" was. The article said I'd ripped your clothes off, but I didn't remember doing that. It said I'd attacked a security guard until he'd had to fire shots in the air, and that I was cursing bad-words like there was no tomorrow. Lies, all lies. People were laughing at me behind my back, I knew, and I wondered what they said about you.

Carlton stayed, and eventually went back to being his discreet self, sanity regained. I know that in his way he loves me. When I had my lump removed five years ago, he was there in the hospital every day, as considerate as could be. Every Sunday morning now, he wakes up and makes me breakfast, frying eggs, toasting bread, and boiling tea. So I should be grateful to you for sending him back that night, Dulcinea Evers, and I would have been, if in all the years since then you hadn't been there between us, in his dreams and in the way he looked at himself in the mirror. We couldn't get rid of you.

Now you're gone. What I've wished for so long has finally happened. But I feel no joy. And it's hard to watch Carlton's stupid grief. He's getting old. There'll be retirement in a few years, and I wonder what we'll do with ourselves then. He thinks I don't know, but I know he went to your funeral, while I stayed home staring at your picture in the paper and trying to see behind your laughing eyes. Was there pain there, too, Dulcinea Evers? From the newspaper, you stared at me and through me, and I felt my small soul laid bare. I thought of your eyes as they looked at me that day on the bank steps: the shock, confusion and hurt, but total lack of fear.

As I gazed at your photograph, I felt the most profound shame. I wanted to cry for the both of us, for you and me. But I didn't.

CHAPTER FIVE

JOSH SCARBINSKY

West Palm Beach, Florida

The Times wanted me to do your obit, Cinea, but even when I got over the shock, I still had to say no. Whoever wrote it, though, did a great job, but it was clear he knew only the paintings, not the girl, not the woman. I am the only one who knew all of you, no matter what Cheryl might think. She sent me an e-mail two days ago, out of the blue, saying that she'd got my address from *The Times* and would I help her in doing something for you. She wants me to meet her in New York. But why should I do that? I've managed to clear you out of my life, Cinea, and now here you are trying to seep in again through the cracks, bringing everything, everything back.

I saw you for the first time walking down Riverside Drive, and I can remember every detail as if it were yesterday. I'd just done a guest lecture at Columbia University, teaching a class of journalism hopefuls how to write art criticism, and I'd decided to take a relaxing stroll along the park. You were ahead of me and I quickly became mesmerized, hypnotized because I'd never before seen anyone walk quite the way you did; I wondered how many years it had taken you to perfect that swinging of the hips to the left and the right. The motion sent out a danger signal, and I should've been warned. But like the other fools on the street that day, I couldn't stop staring – watching you and the people watching you.

Some of the guys who went past weren't just satisfied with slit-eyed sideways glances. No, several of them made 180-degree turns just to have a better look. A few whistled, and I wondered if you smiled or just stared straight ahead. I couldn't tell from gazing at your back.

You turned onto 113th, heading for Broadway, and I followed, marvelling at how well your green print dress outlined your ass. I trailed you for three blocks until you stopped in front of a glass window, seemingly admiring something on display. Suddenly you pushed open the door and went in. There was a painting in the window, and I read the sign above the door: Guacha Gallery. Well, that was my business: looking at art, talking about art, writing articles on art; so I entered as well.

I felt momentarily disoriented as I stepped in, suddenly confronted by the huge canvases on the walls. So much colour and so many faces. It was like wandering into an asylum where everyone was insanely dressed and wanted to have perverse fun with you.

It took me a while to realize someone was talking to me. "She's brilliant, isn't she?"

"What?" I looked at the man hovering at my side. He had a squarish open face, short blond hair and amused blue eyes.

"I am Paul," he said. "I run the gallery. Would you like me to show you around? We have a new exhibition on, and you're in luck because the artist herself just walked in. The opening is tonight."

I looked around but couldn't see that tantalizing green dress anywhere, so I stuck out my hand. "I am Josh Scarbinsky. I teach art history at NYU."

"Hey," he exclaimed, grasping my hand. "I know that name. I've seen some of your articles in the newspaper. You've written a couple of books, haven't you?"

I felt pleased but tried not to show it.

"Yes, I write a bit every now and then," I muttered with suitable humility.

"I'm sure Cinea would love to meet you. I think she's in the office. I'll just get her."

While he was gone, I looked at your paintings and couldn't quell the feeling of disturbance. They all had a wild, wicked energy, with their bold lines and vibrating colours. I thought of Frida Kahlo, Miró, that Indian artist Amrita Shergill. I wondered where you were from. Probably South America, I thought, and you probably were an arrogant, unpleasant person when you weren't painting. I felt an abrupt urge to leave the gallery, but you had appeared.

"Hello, I'm Cinea." Your voice was low and slightly husky, as if you smoked, and the light-brown, almond-shaped eyes were wide and inviting. You smiled at me.

"Yes, well, hello," I garbled, feeling a foolish grin paste itself on my face. "I was just admiring your work. Quite impressive, I must say."

I hadn't expected you to be so young. You could easily have been one of my clueless grad students. As you stood there I had a fleeting fantasy of you standing nude in the living room of my apartment, surrounded by your crazy paintings.

"Are you coming to the opening later?"

"Ah, yes. He… ah… mentioned it…"

"Paul?"

"Yes, Paul. He said the opening is tonight. Do I need an invitation?"

"I'm inviting you." Your gaze was so direct that I felt myself looking away.

"Well, I would love to come. I don't have any classes this evening."

"Where do you teach?" you asked.

"I teach art history at NYU."

"Oh, then you must come," you chuckled. "This is right down your street. Look, I have to do a few last-minute things, but see you later?"

"You bet!" I said, before I had time to phrase a less eager reply. You loped back to your lair, hips moving left and right.

After leaving the gallery, I phoned the newspaper to tell them I'd be writing something about an amazing new artist, and the arts editor must have heard the unusual enthusiasm in my voice because she said that she, too, would come to the opening if she had time.

But you really didn't need me to do any publicity because the gallery was packed that night, and the air buzzed with expectation. Paul heightened your allure by providing island food: jerk chicken, rice and beans, curried mutton. The cocktails all had rum, lots of rum, and as soon as a glass became empty, Paul's jovial hired waiters were there to serve another. No one wanted to leave.

At 10 o'clock, three hours after the party had started, and after Paul had given his little speech about the "greatest discovery in art" since he had entered the business, we were all still there, drunk and in love with you. Well, all of us except my editor Susie, who came late and left soon afterwards. I could see that she disliked you instantly from the stiffening of her face as she looked you up and down. Susie, with her stiff shirt-blouses, tailored pants and dozens of failed relationships, couldn't abide women like you. Still, she emitted grudging admiration when she examined your paintings. There was just no way to deny your talent, and I knew she was going to run my article.

Wealth dripped from a lot of the other guests, men and women slightly past their prime. I'd seen their like at so many *vernissages*. They already had every material thing and were now pursuing the religion of art. Many of them were bankers, you told me, because Paul had been in that business himself before he gave it all up to devote himself to collecting, then buying and selling. He travelled to Latin America and the islands to find pieces his clients couldn't live without, but he hadn't needed to travel to find you. You'd walked into his gallery one day with photographs of your work, and he found himself saying yes yes yes. He obviously still had a banker's brain, though, because his commission was a whopping fifty percent. You told me this gaily when I asked the vulgar question: how much does he take? You didn't seem to care. And tonight, Paul went around quietly placing "sold" stickers next to the paintings while the rest of us basked in reflected glory.

Quite a few people who looked to be about your age were there at the opening, perhaps as much for the free food as for a real appreciation of the work. You kept returning to the side of a slim young woman who went from painting to painting, scrutinizing each intently. As I trailed behind the two of you, you finally introduced her as your best friend, Cheryl, who was in town for a few days. She was pretty in a low-key sort of way, despite a rather prominent nose, and she wore a loosely cut, dark printed dress which seemed a bit too sombre for the occasion. You, meanwhile, could have just stepped from one of your canvases, in your strapless red-and-white dress (hibiscus flowers against a white background), a dress that outlined your body and was just waiting to be peeled off. Yet you looked unbelievably classy.

When the party finally wound down and only the three of us were left with Paul, I invited you all back to my apartment. Cheryl promptly declined, saying she was tired, and Paul said he had things to do. I was elated, thinking I'd have you to myself, but you opted to go home with Cheryl, leaving me to curse in the cab all the way back to my apartment.

Cheryl soon left New York, however, and the weekend that she flew back to Kingston was the first that you spent with me. We got out of bed only to eat and shower.

Within a month, I'd invited you to move in with me, and I gave away furniture in the two-bedroom apartment so that you could have a studio. I wanted you to be happy and, in the days after you moved in, I'd race back uptown between classes to see how you were doing. Sometimes when I returned you weren't in, and other times, you were busy painting and didn't feel like talking.

One evening in bed, you casually mentioned that your visa was running out, and I knew I had to marry you or risk seeing you pack up and leave. I rushed off the next day with our birth certificates and passports to get a license, and two weeks later we had a quiet ceremony at City Hall with only Cheryl and Paul as witnesses, because that's how you wanted it. When we went out to lunch after the "wedding", I got drunk on too much Merlot.

It all seems like details from a painting now, Cinea – a painting whose every feature I know, and yet I can't stop returning to stand in front of it and stare. I keep trying to see beyond the lines and the colours, trying to find the key to your power. Your real talent was making people lose all sense of pride, of self, turning us into slaves. Where did it come from? I would have given up my job and become a worthless bum just to sit and watch you paint, watch the layers adding up, see the specks of light you created with seemingly careless flicks of your brush.

"Here, you try it," you told me once, handing me the brush so that I could add strokes of yellow to the bright-orange bird of paradise flowers you had just finished. But I was petrified. What if I ruined it?

"Don't be so stiff," you said. "It's only paint. I can cover the whole thing again if I want."

You lit a cigarette and sat down, and although I hated the

smell of the smoke and wanted to leave the room, I dutifully followed your instructions. I smiled as the canvas gradually filled with light. "You're doing just great," you said, encouragingly, but after fifteen minutes you left the room to go and take a nap. My arm grew tired, too, and I put the brush in a jar of turpentine. I didn't need an excuse to join you in bed.

But that time you really were asleep. You always said that painting made you exhausted, and now I could understand. I had started perspiring just from the strokes I'd made.

I watched you sleep, looking so vulnerable, and I wanted to cuddle you, fuck you, beat you. I wanted to take off my clothes and wrap you in them to keep you safe. You had turned me into an idiot.

But did *you* ever feel that way about anyone, Cinea? Certainly not me, right? Maybe Cheryl. You needed her so much, but when I once asked if you were in love with her, you just laughed.

"I grew up with five brothers," you said. "Cheryl is the only sister I know."

I didn't believe you. I don't understand that kind of sisterhood, not linked by blood.

I have a sister, too. You met her a few times. She lives in New Jersey, and she has her life and I have mine. We talk on the phone once or twice a month, and we see each other every year-end, for the family get-together at my mother's house. I couldn't comprehend why you needed Cheryl so much – she with her all-seeing eyes and shy, distant smile. If you bought a new blouse you had to get on the phone to regale her with the news. What did you tell her about me, I wonder?

I knew she felt sorry for me; I could feel it. For her it must have been like watching a child play with fire and not being able to pull him away or put it out. And yet sometimes I actually liked her because she was genuine and she loved you. When she came to visit and I took both of you out to dinner, she and I talked about art, both of us so enthralled by what you did, perhaps because we ourselves couldn't draw a straight line. Once, at Lutèce restaurant, Cheryl burst out laughing when I quoted: *Who can, do; who can't, teach; and who can't teach, paint pictures.* You looked at her in surprise, a smile brightening your own face, when the moment before your eyes had been blank with boredom. You got up from the table and said you were going to the ladies' room. As you passed Cheryl's chair, you bent down and hugged her from behind, and she squeezed your arm. In a minute she followed you to the bathroom, and I was left sitting there, a sagging forlorn fool, wondering if sisters always took a piss together. I asked you this question the next day. You sighed and said: "Oh God, man, don't be so small." And, yes, I felt about five inches high.

Cheryl's visits irritated me in the end. I didn't see why she couldn't have stayed at a hotel, but you insisted that she had to stay with us and, when I came home and found you two talking and laughing, I felt I didn't belong in my own place. Neither of you seemed interested in what I had to say. You invited her up for every little event, and I found myself making sarcastic comments. "That's the trouble with teaching," I said once. "Too many damn holidays." But Cheryl didn't take offence. She replied softly, "No, not enough," and I was left trying to figure out what that meant.

Cheryl slept on the inflatable mattress in your studio when she came, and sometimes you would fall asleep there as well, leaving me to myself in our bedroom. You two apparently had so much to talk about that you also had to share her bed, yakking late into the night as if you were on some teenage sleepover. You were both over twenty, for goodness sake! I tried to bite my tongue, but the angry sarcastic words kept coming, and I couldn't hide the jealousy.

"I don't see what your problem is," you told me, looking

truly baffled. "Cheryl and I shared a bed for more than two years when I stayed in her dorm room. Would you prefer if it was a man? What do you imagine we're doing?"

I could have told you what filled my imagination, but I thought it best to keep quiet. I didn't want you to move out, although I probably already knew that there was no keeping you.

Still, when your papers came through and you decided to leave, I was furious. I could've killed you, Cinea. I threatened to tell immigration that the marriage had been a sham, and worse, but you offered to give up the green card, to leave all your paintings behind, and to go back to the island.

"It's not about us," you said. "I need space."

I had no arguments left. I had to let you go.

So, no, I don't believe I'll travel to New York to meet Cheryl. She can do whatever she wants on her own. I don't need you blowing into my face, clouding my eyes again.

I have a real life now, Cinea. I have a girlfriend who loves me, and I'm writing about art again. Last year I took all your paintings down from my walls, because I got tired of your brightness and because my girlfriend, Eva, hated them. I've finally succeeded in letting you go.

CHAPTER SIX

SUSIE, ARTS AND LEISURE EDITOR

New York

It's women like you who cause problems for everyone, Cinea Verse aka Dulcinea Evers. I'd always disliked your type, going around swinging your hips and sticking out your chest, flirting with men and women alike. You revelled in attention. Is that why you decided to end things, because the attention had begun waning? Your friend who called me long-distance a few days ago for Josh's contact details said it was cancer. I didn't say a word. In the obit, we had put "following a short illness".

You know, the only difference between you and your flirtatious sisters – most of whom grow old and washed-out still believing they have gorgeous bodies and irresistible smiles – is that you were talented, Cinea. I'll give you that. But every New York waitress and cab driver has talent. All they need is someone to write about it.

And we, the hacks, need to fill pages, don't we? So when someone like you comes along, we fall over our feet running to write down your words, to snap pictures of you looking like a work of art beside your work of art. We expect insightful utterances and, if you can't provide them spontaneously, we rephrase our questions and redesign your words on the computer screen.

But you never really had a lot to say, did you, Cinea? You

made no obvious attempt to be "media-friendly". Still, perhaps the what-you- see-is-what-you-get image was just that, an image. I'll never know.

When you'd established yourself as a painter that every celeb had to have on his or her wall – I hear that Oprah owns five of your pieces – I invited you to lunch for an interview. You turned up dressed in black leather trousers and a midriff-baring tee-shirt as if you were some sort of pop star, and you dangled a cigarette which a waiter quickly instructed you to extinguish. Eyes followed your movements as you walked to my table, and I could see how much you enjoyed the curious stares. Looking at you, I felt old at 39.

You sat down, crossed your legs, gave me a wide smile and said, "Josh used to talk about you all the time. He said you were the best writer he knew."

I could feel myself blushing and words failed me. Poor Josh. I wondered then how he was getting along in Florida. The paper hadn't heard from him in a while.

"Have a look at the menu, and see if there's anything you like," I said. "I can suggest the grilled filet of sole."

I knew I sounded patronizing but I couldn't help it. I hoped you didn't think I was racist.

We got round to the interview after the waiter brought us drinks – a diet Coke for me and Perrier for you.

Q: *Right. So, who are your influences?*
A: You can write Bob Marley or even Yellowman if you like. Shaggy, Ziggy and Shabba are also good. And Burning Spear.

Q: *But these aren't painters, are they? I mean, did Bob Marley paint?*
A: No, but I listen to a lot of music when I'm working.

You said "working" without the least sign of embarrassment. What **I** did was work – writing down your words. What you did was more like self-entertainment.

You began quizzing me about what kind of music I liked and whether I ever went out to clubs. "We should go together some time," you said airily, your brown eyes alight with some inner joke. I quickly brought the subject back to your "work".

Q: Why do you use such bright colours?
A: I grew up in a bright place. Where did you grow up?

Q: London. Not that bright. Do you return home often, for inspiration?
A: Not really. I love New York and I honestly don't like to travel.

Q: You're joking! I would've thought you'd love to fly. So where do you get ideas for your paintings?
A: From all the people I've known. I grew up surrounded by interesting people.

Q: But there is an insane aspect to many of the characters in your paintings. Did you grow up near a mental hospital?

You burst out laughing.

A: The whole island is a mental hospital, but please don't write that.

Of course, I would.

Q: Has living in New York changed the way you paint?
A: Well, it's easier to buy art materials here.

You giggled, although I didn't see the joke.

Q: You've been very prolific. How long does it take you to complete a painting?
A: It depends. A week. Two weeks. And the oil needs to dry as well.

Q: Your pastel drawings have become popular in the last couple of years, nearly as much as your oil paintings. Why do you use the media that you do?

A: I like the smell of paint. No, seriously, oils give you a luminous kind of quality and great texture. And pastels are just fun. Like being a kid again.

Q: Okay. Let's talk about your background. Do you come from an art-loving family?

For the first time, your supreme self-confidence seemed a bit shaken.

A: Well, my father likes books and music. I don't think he knows much about art. And I've never really discussed art appreciation with my mother or brothers. Do people sit around talking about art in your family?

Q: As a matter of fact, we sometimes do. If your family didn't provide moral support, did you have a mentor? An art teacher at school perhaps? A friend or a husband?

A: Well, my friend Cheryl let me stay and paint in her room when she was a student at university. That's how it all started. I couldn't go home at the time for various reasons and I shared her room for about two years. All I did was paint – well, along with a few other things. Is that what you would call a mentor?

I waited for you to mention Josh, but you didn't and I wasn't going to.

Q: Didn't it get small in the student room, with you, your friend and your paintings?

A: Not that I remember. Cheryl went home to her aunt's house most weekends, and sometimes I went with her. Besides if we had an argument or if she had to study, she usually went over to her cousin's room. He was also a student on campus.

Q: *What a cosy arrangement. You all must have had such fun.*
A: Yes, it was fun.

Q: *Is it hard being taken seriously as a woman artist?*

You sipped your water, sucked on a piece of ice as if it were candy, and finally answered.

A: Nobody takes women seriously. Not even other women.

You stared at me, smiling in your coy, annoying way. Okay, touché. Now, I was going to have to write an article showing that I at least took you seriously.

We went on with this game for a good while, and it was like talking with an impish child. When you eventually got bored, you said: "Look, just write what you want. Be creative. I think you know me well enough."

"That would be unethical," I replied. Furthermore, I didn't know you at all.

But there weren't going to be any more revelations because now you were getting all excited about dessert. "I love brownies," you declared. "Mmm. My favourite colour."

I had to laugh. As we left the restaurant together, I reminded you that a photographer would come to your studio later that day. You nodded, your thoughts seeming far away. We shook hands, and I strode off in the opposite direction, turning only once to look back. You were still standing in front of the restaurant, puffing on a new cigarette and staring into space.

I heard from you a week later when you phoned to thank me for the "lovely" article I'd written about your work.

"I never realized I was so intelligent," you said, laughing.

Then you repeated your casual invitation: "Let's go out again sometime, for real."

But you swam in waters that were way too uncertain for me, Cinea, and I have a deep fear of drowning. Besides, although I appreciated you more after the interview, I still didn't like your type.

I will write one more article about you, however, because this scattering of your ashes sounds like a good story. "An Artist Returns Home: On a windy day in Riverside Park, Cinea Verse is saying hello again to the city she loved." It's already written, my dear.

CHAPTER SEVEN

CHERYL

New York

I'm shaking with nervousness and hunger by the time we land at JFK. It's strange to be back in New York without you waiting for me, Dulci – like running into a school playground after sundown, when everyone else has gone home. I try not to cry as I stride into the sterile new terminal, just ahead of Danny. The place is a big change from the dingy hall of my early visits, when panting dogs would be waiting to sniff at disembarking passengers. Do you remember how I used to complain and curse about that? And you would laugh and say: "Well, sweetheart, move to a country where certain plants don't grow and you won't have dogs sniffing at your you-know-what." Of course, you yourself weren't against these certain plants, and that was part of the problem.

The dogs didn't stop the trade, though, did they? We are an inventive nation and will always find a hiding-hole. And now there are much worst things than ganja to worry about, things concealed where the customs people can never find them, in heads and hearts. I can still hear your frantic voice when you called me that day to tell me the shocking news. Someone you knew, another artist, had been in one of the buildings and hadn't made it out. But not even that grief or the smell of burning that hung over the city for weeks could bring you back home.

The lines are moving quickly in the terminal today, as the human-traffic police direct "citizens" to one end and visitors to the other. On our side of the terminal, they give us curt instructions on which queues to join.

"This way. Line number 4. You – line number 7."

"Don't forget which finger to give for the fingerprinting," Danny whispers behind me. I smile.

"Hi," I say, as I walk up to the immigration box, with the officer sitting on her high stool. She has long frizzy hair, a sharp nose and unfriendly eyes.

"Passport," she demands loudly.

I hand it over, along with the Arrival-Departure form where I'd ticked "no" to a long list of questions such as: *Do you have any live animals in your luggage*, and *Are you carrying any chemical substances*. I wonder how your ashes would be classified, Dulci?

"Put your thumb here," Frizzy barks.

I lift my left hand.

"No, your right thumb first," she says impatiently.

I stare at her. It must be difficult to do this kind of thing all day, every day.

"What's the purpose of your visit?"

"A funeral," I reply, opting for the truth without further explanation. You've already had your funeral, Dulci; this is more your idea of fun – half of you in New York and half on the island.

Frizzy passes back the documents. "Next," she bellows, without looking at me again.

I move towards the customs area, walking slowly so that Danny can catch up.

"So you're not a terrorist and me neither," he remarks when he joins me. "Now I just hope they don't find the yellow yam and green bananas in me bag."

He grins at me, and I know that he is joking. But you can never be sure what people will pack, Dulci, because the customs hall is reeking with the smell of rum; somebody's well-wrapped bottle hasn't survived the impact of being carelessly thrown onto the conveyor belt. Danny inhales deeply and bursts out laughing, and suddenly a blonde, pallid-skinned customs officer, bulging out of her uniform, is barring our way.

"Are you travelling together?" she asks, a hand on each side of her large abdomen.

"Not really. We met on the plane," I say.

"What's in the bags?"

"Clothes and bits and pieces," I answer. The bits and pieces are you, Dulci, sorry; I don't want to start talking about ashes.

"What's your profession?"

"I teach mathematics at the Omega Convent of Mercy High School in Kingston," I enunciate primly. She hesitates and then waves me through. But Danny is going to get the treatment. I walk a short distance away and watch as the woman doggedly goes through his suitcase, holding up each item of underwear and flapping the garment about in the rum-soaked air. When she is through, Danny takes his time meticulously refolding his clothes and replacing them in his bag. He whistles as he works, and I recognize the melody of "I shot the Sheriff". It's an unnecessary provocation, and just the kind of thing you yourself might have done, Dulci. I wonder why I'm even waiting for him.

"Man, you saw how much she liked me briefs," he says when he walks up. "Just imagine her fantasies tonight, my God!"

"I'm just glad I didn't give you my friend's ashes," I reply. "That woman would've carted you off for sure if she'd found the bottle."

"You're right. And it's a good thing you're a teacher. I should've said pastor instead of auto-parts dealer when she asked."

"Yes, you definitely look like you've just stepped out of a church."

He laughs. "So where are you going now?"

"I have to get a taxi to Manhattan."

I plan to be in New York for three days, Dulci. Sprinkle your ashes with Josh tomorrow (if he turns up), meet with lawyers the next day and leave the day after.

"My mother should be outside waiting," Danny says. "Why don't you come home with us and have some food, then I can take you to your hotel?"

"That's too much trouble for you."

"Lawd, girl. Stop you foolishness. Let me decide what is trouble. Or you have a man coming to meet you?"

"No man," I say as I walk with him to the exit.

★

Danny's mother looks not a day over fifty, Dulci. She must have had him when she was fifteen or something. She is waiting for us in a spanking new SUV and, when we approach, she descends to give her son a big hug. Then she turns to me and does the same, wrapping her arms around me as I hold onto my bags, so that I feel like a lamp post. It always surprises me when people you don't know from Adam are so effusive. But you were also like that at times, Dulci – a member of the instant-friend, hug-and-move-on society.

She is wearing high heels, tight green pants and a matching fitted blouse. Her dark brown hair has streaks of gold, and her fingernails and toenails are polished an attractive burgundy. Everything about her shouts that she is a woman who takes care of herself.

"Moms, this is Cheryl," Danny says. "She's coming home with us for a bite so I hope you've cooked something nice."

"Don't I always cook something nice? Happy to have you with us, sweetheart," she says to me. "My name is Gwen,

70

since Danny forgot to tell you." She laughs at her son, who is busy putting our bags in the back of the vehicle.

"Mommy, I'll drive," he says when he is done. "I have a feeling that Cheryl doesn't like speed."

"But just listen to this bwoy, eh?" Gwen winks at me. "I am the slowest driver in America!"

Danny throws back his head and laughs. "Right, Moms. That's a good one."

"So how was the flight?" Gwen asks when we're on the road.

"No problem at all," Danny responds. "But I got searched as usual when we landed. The customs woman held up all me underpants for everybody to see."

"Well, what you expect when you dress like that? I keep telling you to wear nice shirt and proper shoes. Nobody would think you're a successful businessman by the way you dress. Clothes make the man, you know. Nothing is truer than that."

"What, you want me to wear suit and tie just to fly?"

"No, I'm only saying you should take more care with your appearance. Look how nice Cheryl looks. I bet they didn't search her."

"That's because she tell them she is a teacher," Danny retorts.

"So, I don't look nice?" I ask, teasingly. "That's not what you said on the plane."

"Oh, so he was sweet-talking you?" Gwen says. "I'm not surprised. I don't know when he's going to settle down and get married. How about you, Cheryl? Are you married, sweetheart?"

"Of course she's not married, Mommy. What a question!"

I smile and keep quiet, Dulci. They probably would stop the car and put me out on the road, if they knew. Even you were shocked when I told you everything just before you went – and all that time I thought you'd suspected, that you knew about me tiptoeing in the dark.

Gwen lives in the Bronx, in an area of tree-lined roads and two-storey houses. She and Danny occupy the two top floors and rent out the basement for extra money, she tells me as we enter. The living room is nicely furnished with white sofas and a glass-topped coffee table. Magazines of every kind, alongside books on nursing, are stacked on a long, low bookshelf against one wall. In the dining room, a highly polished mahogany table has been set for two, but Gwen quickly gets busy adding a third place.

"I hope you like stew peas," she says. "And I hope you don't mind lots of pepper."

"Mmm, sounds good," I reply, smiling. Christ, another pepper-lover! I feel so uncomfortable, Dulci. I wish I had gone straight to the hotel where I could be alone with you. I set my bag with your ashes carefully down in a corner and ask Gwen where I can wash my hands. Danny points me to the bathroom before she answers. It's shiny clean in there, as if everything has been scrubbed earlier today. I look at myself in the mirror as I soap my hands – trying to get rid of the grime of travel – and even to myself I look tired. I examine my eyes as the tears come, noting the redness from lack of sleep. I watch the water roll down, and I hear the faint drip as the tears hit the sink. I need to weep for you, Dulci, but you're always laughing, telling me to stop the foolishness, that there's no reason to cry.

I rinse my hands and face, and dry up with one of the soft, sweet-smelling pink towels that are neatly folded on a wicker stand. I look at my watch; it's only three-thirty in the afternoon, but this morning in Kingston already seems like a lifetime ago.

Throughout our late lunch, Gwen tells snippets of her life: how she had Danny when she was seventeen and didn't have enough money to take care of him. How she went to work as a maid in New York, leaving him with her mother. How nearly every week she sent him clothes and toys. How each year she wanted to return home but couldn't find either the time or the money. How she wanted to bring him to New York but didn't believe she could work and take care of him at the same time. How she studied to be a nurse in the evenings and now earns a good salary caring for old people in an "assisted facility".

"I knew he was better off with my mother," she sighs. "I'm just glad he realizes that I did what I did because I loved him." She reaches across the table and holds Danny's hand, and he lets her. I think of Aunt Mavis: I can't remember a time when she touched either Trev or me like that. Still, she never left us. She was always there, like the sun behind dark clouds. She shone only when you were around, Dulci. Of the three of us (not counting Pepper), I think she loved you the most, and you weren't even her flesh and blood.

It's past six in the evening now, and we are still exchanging stories. I tell them about you, Dulci, about the good times at Omega Academy, about living together on campus, and about your life in New York. And guess what? Gwen remembers seeing you on Oprah, when you did that per-formance showing how anybody can paint if they want to.

"That was your friend?" Gwen says, eyes wide. "What a beautiful girl. She gave Oprah a brush and showed her how to fill up the canvas, and then they had people come up from the audience to do the same thing. You know, I even thought about taking an art class afterwards but never got round to it. I'm so sorry to hear she passed away. Poor child. So many young people dying now of cancer."

I nod. The exhaustion I feel is suddenly overwhelming and all I want to do is sleep.

"Thanks for everything," I say, smiling at both of them.

"I wish I could stay longer but I have to go to the hotel now. I have a lot to do tomorrow."

"Will the hotel charge a fee if you don't show up?" Gwen asks.

"No, I don't think so. Why?"

"Then just call them and cancel. You can stay here. I'll fix up the bed in the guest-room." She goes off.

"Boy, your mother is bossy, isn't she?"

"Been in America too long," Danny grins.

I'm falling asleep before I know it, Dulci, in Gwen's bed with the pink floral bedspread. It's the girliest room I've ever slept in, like something out of a catalogue, with stuffed dogs and teddy bears everywhere.

And I dream about you, that you're in my room on campus painting, and telling me why you paint. We're laughing at some joke when suddenly your father bursts in with a knife and starts slashing at the canvases. You scream at him to stop and I jump up from my chair and grab at his arm. He turns on me, and the knife flashes through the air. My blood spurts out onto one of your canvases, and we all watch in awe as the liquid shapes itself into a hibiscus flower. As your father stares at the image, stupefied, you and I collapse on the floor, giggling like little girls.

"The damn fool," you whisper to me, and I laugh hysterically, my hand over the knife wound in my chest.

I wake up, still laughing. I don't know where I am.

"You all right?" someone asks in the darkness. "You were screaming and then you started laughing like a madwoman." It's Danny, standing in the doorway.

"Weird dream," I mutter, embarrassed.

I reach over and turn on the bedside light, closing my eyes against the brightness. When I open them again, Danny is still there, wearing pyjama trousers, his chest bare.

"What time is it?" I ask, for something to say.

"About 11:30. I was just going to bed."

He gazes at me and I stare back, nervous and excited although I don't want to be. His body seems completely relaxed as he walks towards the bed, as if this is all inevitable. When he lies down beside me, I reach over and switch off the lamp.

Everything about him feels so different from Trev's tightness, Dulci, but I can't shake the pain of my own betrayal, an ache that reaches to my bones.

Trev must have been seventeen and me sixteen when I saw him naked on his bed, his body thrusting against the mattress, the muscles standing out in his back and buttocks. I'd wanted to tell him something and had entered his room without knocking, and there he was. My breath caught in my throat as I stopped short in the doorway, forgetting what I'd come to say. He looked up and our eyes locked. I felt myself moving towards him.

Now it seems as if all the years since then have been spent creeping around in the night so as not to wake Aunt Mavis, and looking past each other in the daylight. It was such a relief to escape to you in New York, Dulci.

Yet, you were so shocked when I told you. Or you pretended to be.

"I knew you were close but not *that* close," you laughed weakly the day before you went. "I should have guessed, though."

You scrutinized my face for a long time, with a strange smile, until I grew uneasy.

"I'm used to seeing every little thing about people and filing it away for the next painting, and you're used to looking at figures and adding everything up in your head, and yet neither of us saw what was right in front of us for so long," you mused.

It was your turn to tell me your secret. And I cried like a

child because I should have known but didn't. Yes, I can add, subtract, multiply and divide, and the answer will always be the same. I don't have the imagination to mess with the equation.

"When did you realize?" I asked.

"When you had dengue fever. Remember?"

I remembered.

So much can happen in two years, Dulci, and so little. Sometimes I think we were hardly together in my dorm room because I had classes for most of the day; we ate our meals in the cafeteria; we watched TV in the common room; and so many nights I stayed with Trev.

Other times, it seems that we were always with each other, always laughing about something, always talking about something. That week, for instance, when I was down with dengue fever, you seemed not to have left my side for a second; you fed me mashed up food, made me drink coconut water and helped me to the bathroom. You sponged my body with a wet washcloth, for minutes at a time, trying to cool the fever and stem the delirium. For four or five days, the soothing washcloth moved over my breasts, my abdomen, my thighs. Did I take your hand, Dulci? Did I say *Don't do that, never stop*, what?

When the virus was defeated, and we'd invested in a mosquito net, I thought everything had been part of my fevered imagination. I never mentioned it, and you said nothing until the end.

Now lying here with Danny, thinking of Trev, and remembering your touch, I don't know who I am anymore, or where you stop and I begin.

CHAPTER EIGHT

MAVIS

Kingston

Trevor came over to eat dinner with me earlier this evening, looking like someone who'd just heard that his mother had died. Sadder, probably, because I can't imagine he would be that down in the dumps if I should kick the bucket. His mind seemed miles away, and I guess he was missing Cheryl. Or maybe he was thinking of you, Dulcinea.

None of us has been the same since we heard the news. The whole neighbourhood has been chattering about how beautiful you were, even those who only saw you from a distance in the street, even those who used to mutter that you "show off just like you father". They always expected you to come back, but I knew you were gone to stay. It was the only way.

That's what I try to tell your mother when she comes to sit on the verandah with me, wringing her hands and crying about what she should have done. You had to go, Dulcinea, and it's not your fault that everybody now wants to scream their pain. Except for my son, that is, who has little to say.

In fact, Trevor hardly said a word as we ate. I couldn't blame him. Silence is natural to us now, even though I've been trying to force the words out since your funeral. But my throat has gone rusty, refusing to obey me.

You were the only one who understood me without the

words, Dulcinea. You felt my curse just as I felt your gift. Both were waiting to be unleashed. Being able to see, really to see, is the worst kind of curse, my dear, and sometimes you have to give up another sense in exchange; sometimes you have to stop talking, hearing or touching.

At least you had an outlet. You could draw. Everything you saw you put on paper, and that freed you. I could do nothing with my curse, except to try and run from it. All my life I tried to escape until finally I had to give in or go mad. Pepper knew it, you felt it, and the children suffered from it – this affliction of seeing. When your father, that stupid man, put your clothes outside, you kept your head high and stepped firmly onto your path. You gave me the courage to do the same, a tough-back woman like me, who has seen so much.

The visions began when I was about six, Dulcinea: visions of car crashes, drownings, murders, you name it. They came both when I was asleep and when I was awake. When I slept, I woke up screaming. When I was awake, I tried to squeeze myself into a ball, with my head between my knees. Everyone said I was a strange child. They told my mother to take me to Bellevue Hospital to get my head examined. But my mother knew. Her grandfather had been a seer, the most famous obeah man on the island in the last century, and he'd passed his "talent" down to her mother, and now to me. But why me? Why couldn't it have been my sister, Annette? She got the beauty while I got the "gift", my grandmother would tell me later, as if this were some kind of comfort, as if one shouldn't have both. I wish she could've met you, Dulcinea, because I would have said: See? It's possible.

But do you know what it's like to want to bang your head on the wall just to stop the whisperings? Or to stay up as late as you can just so you won't have to dream? If someone was going to die in our neighbourhood, I knew it first. In the beginning I told my mother, but she couldn't handle the fear. I could see the dread in her eyes when I described my visions. She was afraid for me and of me, as if I was somehow responsible for the family burden. I think she would have preferred another kind of affliction – polio, whooping cough, blindness – anything but this.

If you could paint my life, Dulcinea, how would you do it? You were so fond of bright colours, even in the clothes you wore, that you'd probably have trouble finding the shades of black, grey and blue to show my fears. But I *will* give you colour, darling, enough to last forever.

Let's start with Canvas Number One. Sketch a family, Dulcinea – mother, father and two daughters. Show them standing in front of a brick house with a wide verandah. The girls are only a year apart in age but miles apart in looks and personality. The younger one has big bright eyes, a glowing smile and shiny curls. She seems destined to become a beauty queen. The older girl has a serious face, and shy manner. Draw her looking at the ground. Don't show her eyes looking out from the canvas or they might scare the viewer. The mother is beautiful, with dark-brown skin and long black hair. Her eyes are luminous – think of wet beach stones. Find a way to show her ancestry, because she descended from the Maroons and was proud of her "pure" African blood. Her people never surrendered, as she repeated time and time again to anyone who would listen; no, they took to the hills and fought so fiercely that the English were forced to sign a peace treaty. She was immensely proud of her heritage, Dulcinea, and she would have done anything for her people, except live with them. Mama was a true city girl; no dark hills for her once she discovered Kingston. The hills lived in me instead.

Draw a slim, medium-height man standing beside her. Try to capture his ancestry, too, as shown in the milk-tea skin and curly, reddish hair – a mixture of Irish and African, although he'd never met the Irish father. Put a pack of Craven A cigarettes in one hand, because he was never without them, and perhaps have a bit of smoke curling up from his lips. Make it real-looking so that people can actually smell the smoke that constantly clung to him. Give him a lopsided smile but also do your best to show the hidden anger that would sometimes flare up for no reason.

Now draw two mango trees peeping from behind the house, if you still have space. You can show their branches and deep-green leaves swaying in the wind above the roof. Fill one tree with enticing yellow fruit and leave the other bare. People may wonder why, but you are the artist, Dulcinea, you can do what you want.

Still, I'll tell you the story about those trees. My father planted them when we moved into that house there on Upper Wellington Road, the first house he'd ever owned. They were East-Indian mango trees, and our mouths watered when we imagined the sweet juicy fruit we would receive.

One tree couldn't wait to grow; it shot up, almost overnight it seemed, and spread its branches across the back yard. The other tree seemed weak and hesitant, its leaves ragged and mildewed. We watched them grow and, within a year, the beautiful tree was laden with fruit – the most delicious, succulent mangoes we'd ever tasted. I can still see Annette and me eating them, licking the nectar that ran down our arms to our elbows, sucking on the seed.

The other tree stubbornly refused to bear fruit. My father gave it several more months and then announced that he would chop it down. But my mother disagreed. "Leave it alone," she told him. "Everything has its use, no matter what we may think." When she said it, she sighed, as if she wasn't talking about the tree, but something else. My father, however, was determined. The infertile tree had to go. He made plans and borrowed tools; he would dismember the tree first from the top, chopping off the branches, and afterwards he would saw through the trunk. The tree's demise was scheduled for a Sunday, but the previous Thursday we got news that a hurricane was approaching and might hit the island. By Friday noon, we had filled up on water and barricaded the windows and doors, and my sister and I stayed home from school. Hurricane Janice hit with force on the Saturday afternoon. It raged through the rest of the day and throughout the night. Annette and I listened to the wind howling and the rain pounding down, and we felt excited and frightened at the same time. We heard things being blown about outside, sometimes slamming into the house, and when I closed my eyes, I could see everything happening. I saw the storm as if I was standing outside in it – the trees being forced to bend until they gave up the struggle; the rain coming down like there was no tomorrow; the swirling brown water racing down the gutters and carrying away everything in its path. The next day there was no surprise for me, but my father was furious when he went out and observed that every plant and every tree in the neighbourhood had been uprooted except the one mango tree he had planned to chop down. It stood there, amidst the devastation, like a mocking duppy, with the fruit of its sister tree scattered all around its base and half buried in the mud. My father ran inside, grabbed his saw and attacked the tree with unthinking ferocity.

"Papa, watch out," I shouted, just as the mango tree flung down one of its hurricane-torn branches. My father sprang back, and the branch missed him by inches.

"I told you to leave it alone," my mother said. "At least it will provide shade. You are lucky that Mavis saw the branch coming down."

I shrugged as my father backed away from the tree, shaking his head. He gave me a strange look and went inside the house. That's the thing about seeing, Dulcinea, you never get any thanks. I could've warned him even before the branch began to fall, but why waste one's breath?

So that's the mango tree; it lived longer than my father but never gave us a single fruit. How do you put that in a painting?

When we moved into the house, we'd also inherited a cotton tree in the furthest corner of the backyard. It had white ragged puffs of cotton that we actually picked every now and then, but my mother told us never to play near the tree after the sun went down. Like everyone else in the neighbourhood, she believed that duppies lived under the cotton tree at night. If she threw water out the back door in the evening, and it inadvertently splashed in the direction of the cotton tree, she would apologise profusely, and we had to do the same: "Sorry, I hope I didn't wet you up". No one wanted to offend the spirits, but I could have told her to throw as much water as she liked, stones even, because if duppies had been there, I would've seen them. But people need their superstitions, don't they, Dulcinea? They need to believe in things that they can't see, and to not believe, at times, what their own eyes tell them.

The cotton tree doesn't have to be in the painting (Hurricane Janice got rid of it anyway), but perhaps you can give the house a certain look, a certain feel, to show the spirits that lived with us – right inside and not out under some tree. My grandmother was one of them; I saw her every night. Whenever I woke up, she was there standing over me, watching. Have you ever known that feeling, Dulcinea, of someone in your room, watching and waiting for who knows what? She was a small, wiry brown woman with perfect white teeth and rough grey hair that she kept in long plaits. I'd seen her in the flesh only twice as a little girl, when my mother took Annette and me to visit her family in the hills. On each occasion, Granny had announced to my mother: "This one has Granddad's eyes. She can see in the night. Send her to live with me when she's older." And my mother looked from me to her and smiled nervously. Mama's greatest wish was for me to be ordinary and here was Granny saying that I was an oddball like her. "Act normal." "Behave normal." Those were the words my mother raised me on. And I really tried to laugh, play and look innocent like Annette, but I couldn't keep up the game for long. Meanwhile, Granny kept her body in the hills and sent her spirit to Kingston to live with us in the house on Upper Wellington Road, waiting for me to shoulder the curse. So, draw a ghostly figure somewhere in your picture, Dulcinea: white dress, big teeth and glowing eyes, if you want to have some fun. But remember, she wasn't even a duppy yet.

Let's use some perspective now for Canvas Number Two and Upper Wellington Road. You could paint the view from the very top of our street, looking all the way down to where you could see the sea, the harbour. This painting must have a touch of nostalgia, something that brings to mind those days of life without television, when people read the one newspaper and listened to one of the two radio stations. And no, you don't have to hold back on the colours. This one can be picturesque, like a postcard that tourists would like. Draw a stretch of houses built off the ground on concrete blocks, with sloping roofs and big verandahs where neighbours gathered on weekends to play dominoes and ludo. Show each house with a good bit of land around it, and add the greens of paw-paw trees, mango, soursop, breadfruit – and the purple of the star-apple. Have you even eaten a star-apple, Dulcinea, and felt your lips sticking together from the gummy juice? I haven't seen one since Trevor and I came here to live with Cheryl and her father, not one. Where have they gone?

Upper Wellington Road was full of trees and plants that grew with renewed vigour after each rainy season. The houses had all been built from scratch, with love; none of this prefabricated concrete stuff that's everywhere now. My father bought Number 12A from a light-skinned family who was moving to England – all eight of them with all their belongings. My father wondered aloud to my mother how they could bear to leave such a beautiful house, but he wished them good luck. The house seemed huge to Annette and me, and the most wonderful thing was that it had an indoor toilet and bathroom. No more trekking outside for a shower or to do one's business. We had three bedrooms, a proper living room, and a big kitchen that looked out on the backyard with its cotton tree. The floors were made of mahogany that Annette and I would have to learn to polish, and the ceilings were high above us. Each house on Upper Wellington seemed more beautiful than the next.

So paint these beloved houses stretching down the road until you get to Lower Wellington where they became more like tenements, with several families to a yard. If you kept going to the end of the road, you'd pass a cigarette factory and finally come to the massive building that everyone in Kingston knew: the General Penitentiary. Our street began with the sprawling green complex of an army camp and ended in a huge prison by the sea, home of notorious murderers such as Rhygin, who had robbed and killed his way across the island and had been captured only after the biggest manhunt anyone could remember.

And not far from the prison, Dulcinea, was the madhouse, Bellevue Hospital, where our neighbours recommended that my mother take me to be examined. It sat on several acres of land, an expansive, ramshackle building with strange unhappy people wandering around. Bellevue was the home of prophets like Alexander Bedford, who'd gathered masses of people to watch him fly to Zion, only to have the government clip his wings and fling him inside the madhouse. Everyone knew it was worse to be there than to be in the General Penitentiary.

The school that my sister and I attended, Wellington Primary and High School, sat opposite Bellevue, and we had a good view of the residents every day. Sometimes they even called out to us as we walked home. "How you do, little girl? What a pretty sister you have!" They always addressed their comments to me. Always to me, as if they and I had something in common, as if we were somehow related, without my knowing it. Or, as if Annette were too precious to be hailed directly.

Things happened on Welllington Road, both Upper and Lower. Soldiers from the army camp sometimes galloped down to the harbour on their imported horses, seeming to be from another world. A prisoner or a madman would escape every now and then, causing widespread fear and trembling. Neighbours quarrelled over domino games and threw things at one another, with the police having to be called. People went for a swim and never returned. Parents died.

I saw shades of it all before it took place, Dulcinea.

Time now for Canvas Number Three. Paint two sisters, aged twelve and eleven, sitting on a church bench. They are wearing black dresses for the first time in their lives. Make one girl's face wet with tears, her eyes overflowing like the Rio Cobre after a flood. Show the other girl dry-faced, staring straight ahead. Use your skills to convey pain beyond tears if you can. And, in the background, paint serious sombre faces, a wooden cross hanging on a wall, and stained glass windows. Here again you can use your bright colours, Dulcinea, as you show the sun streaming through the coloured glass, a conflagration of red, orange and yellow above the heads of the mourners. But don't get carried away because it was a dark occasion, my father's funeral.

I could have got through it okay, though, if it weren't for Annette's constant bawling, her keening in the dark as if her world had ended. I always knew she was his favourite, and she knew it too, but I think he loved me as much as he could, and my pain was just as great as Annette's, except that I couldn't cry. When he'd got sick, coughing day and night, I knew from his first spit that he wouldn't make it. I wanted to share the knowledge with someone, but only Granny was there to shake her head above my bed as if nothing could surprise her. When it came to pass, and Daddy died spitting up blood, I sat in a corner of his room and stared without words or tears.

"That one really strange," the neighbours said. "She never even cry at her father funeral." But the words just bounced off my skin. I heard them but they didn't hurt until much later.

With our father gone, Annette and I felt as if someone had put us in a boat and pushed us out to sea alone. Maybe that's another idea, Dulcinea; paint two girls in a small boat, bobbing on the Caribbean Sea, surrounded by never-ending blue. Adrift, that's what we were, until my mother found the strength to take charge and haul us back to land. She wasn't a Maroon for nothing.

With my father gone, Mama had to start working, and the only job she could get right away was in the cigarette factory, a ten-minute walk to Lower Wellington Road. The factory paid well, but not enough for her to take care of the two of us and herself, plus keep the house. So the decision was made. One of us had to go to live with Granny in Maroon country: me.

Uncle Selwyn, my mother's brother, came to pick me up on a Sunday morning that was warm, bright and silent, with most of our neighbours gone to church or still sleeping, after the late-Saturday-night domino games and rum-drinking.

Annette and I cried and clung to each other outside the house, there on the sidewalk of Upper Wellington Road. I didn't want to let her go – she was my yardstick for normalcy and goodness – but in the end I found myself in my uncle's old Morris Oxford, headed for the hills, to Granny. It was seven months after Daddy died, and I'd just turned thirteen.

Once the car began moving, I didn't look back at Mama and Annette standing at the gate, waving and weeping. I already felt miles away, my future sealed.

"Don't worry," Uncle Selwyn said comfortingly. "You'll love living with your Granny. She's the best cook in the District of Look Behind. You won't want to come back to Kingston."

Yes, that's where Granny lived, in the District of Look Behind, in the Cockpit Country. My mother had explained the meaning of the name to Annette and me.

"The English soldiers who were tracking the Maroons in the 1700s had to keep looking behind them because any moment there could be an ambush. That's how my people stayed free. We used to ambush them and leave just one of them alive to go back and spread the news. So, they finally signed a treaty and left us alone. You know what a treaty is?"

We'd nodded in unison; we'd heard the story a million times before. But Mama would still launch into explanations, getting worked up, saying that the British had promised the Maroons 15,000 acres of land and then given them only 1,500 in the treaty. The British found it hard to accept that these Africans, slaves who had either escaped or been freed by the Spaniards who'd once ruled the island, should live as their own masters. They tried everything to vanquish the Maroons, even shipping hundreds of them off to icy Nova Scotia – from whence the Maroons made their way back to Africa – but in the end freedom prevailed, and my mother was there to tell us all about it.

Uncle Selwyn glanced at his watch and asked me if I knew any jokes. I thought about it but none came to mind.

Uncle Selwyn was my mother's only brother, and although I hadn't seen much of him until now, he'd always brought Annette and me presents and made us laugh on the few occasions when he visited Kingston. He was a coffee farmer in the hills, and very busy, Mama had told us, promising to let us taste coffee when we were older. Up to my departure from home, all we'd ever drunk for breakfast was peppermint tea.

"Can I drink coffee at Granny's house?" I asked my uncle.

"You can drink whatever you want, as long as it's not white rum," he said, filling the car with his laughter. "I grow the best coffee on this island. You know that, right?" I nodded.

We were now driving past the army camp, and Uncle said: "Let me know when you're hungry and we'll make a stop. Your mother put enough food in that basket to feed an army. Maybe we should give the soldiers some." He laughed again, and I smiled in spite of myself.

We were driving north, with the Blue Mountains in front of us and the sea behind. The brightness of the morning almost hurt my eyes, but I felt a sense of elation for the first time, as we headed up Constant Spring Road toward Stony Hill. Uncle Selwyn slowly drove round the bends, passing mansions as well as shacks perched on the slopes, their roofs glinting under the sun. There you are, Dulcinea, Canvas Number Four: a blue car heading up the mountainside, shining in the sunlight, with houses of every colour seeming about to roll down the incline. And you can paint a young girl looking curiously out the car window, wondering what was in store for her.

"We're going to cut through St. Mary and cross St. Ann, before we get to Trelawney," Uncle informed me. "Do you know how many other parishes there are on the island?"

"Yes, eleven more. Fourteen altogether," I said unenthusiastically. Was this going to be a geography lesson?

"Right," Uncle said, and started whistling. I gazed at the deep valley on our right, at the river meandering at the bottom, the water cocoa-brown. I imagined myself lying on my back, looking at the sky, and floating with the river down to the sea.

We reached the District of Look Behind at just after four in the afternoon. Have you ever been to the Cockpit Country, Dulcinea? You, Cheryl and Trevor are city children, growing up with noise and mayhem. The Cockpit Country, where Granny lived, had a beauty and quietness that went straight to your heart. As far as the eye could see were rugged hills – green, blue, orange – and steep plunging valleys. The sky seemed as if you could touch it.

A narrow dirt path led from the small bumpy main road to Granny's house, and I could hear myself breathe as I stepped out of the car. Granny's front yard was filled with purple jacaranda, yellow bougainvillea, red hibiscus and a myriad orchids. To the right side of the house, a flame of the forest tree was in full bloom, its orange flowers like bulbs of fire, commanding me to look at it. The house itself was built from long planks of wood, and seemed to have about four rooms. It was painted green and yellow, with a rusting zinc roof, and you had to climb up three steps to get to the verandah that ran along the front. Outside the yard were more trees and plants, no other house in sight. I felt as if I was seeing all of this for the first time even though I'd been there years before with Mama.

Granny came out to meet us before we got to the front door.

"Mavis, child, you come home!" she said, hugging me. I

hugged her back, without realizing what I was doing. I didn't plan to stay for long.

How would you paint my life with Granny, Dulcinea? How many canvases would you need? How many tubes of white to paint the mist in the mornings, the rain in the afternoons? How many yellows and greens to paint the parrots and all the other birds that flew into our yard when Granny put bits of corn out for them to eat? And what about black, pure black, for the nights, when you couldn't even see your hand in front of your face once the kerosene lamps had been extinguished?

Granny got up every morning before six o'clock, and by the time I awoke, breakfast was already on the table: cornmeal porridge, dumplings, fried plantain, boiled eggs, and bush tea. I'd never realized that tea could come in so many flavours, all plucked from Granny's backyard. If I'd been coughing the night before, I would wake up to fevergrass tea. If it was that time of the month, and I'd complained of cramps, I woke up to ginger tea. Sometimes I longed for Horlicks or Ovaltine, which Mama used to buy. But once Granny had made me her chocolate tea, from grated cocoa lumps, with the oil still swimming on top, it was difficult forever afterwards to drink anything from a can or bottle.

Each morning after breakfast, I walked through the light mist to the outdoor bathroom and stood under an icy stream of water that came through pipes from Granny's well. The water blasted the last vestiges of sleep from my body, and I was then ready for school. I dressed in a blue pleated skirt and white blouse, and walked a mile and a half down the dirt track to another wooden building that served as the school in the District of Look Behind. The only sound that accompanied me on my walk was the call of birds, coming through the withdrawing mist.

The school had put me in Grade 9, and my class had eight

other students, all girls. Two teachers taught us everything – Mr. Robinson for Maths, Science and Religion, and Miss O'Hare for English and History. Mr. Robinson was from Montego Bay, to which he returned every evening, and we'd heard that he was a pastor in some church or other. Miss O'Hare was from Ireland. She had long curly black hair, rosy cheeks and sad brown eyes. Every day, she got us to write stories, which she then read out in class. I wrote funny, absurd stories, as far from my own life as possible. I'd decided that it was nobody's business what went on in my head, Dulcinea. But Miss O'Hare took a liking to me, perhaps because she sensed that I was running away from something, just as she was, or perhaps because my stories made her laugh. I wondered about her family in Ireland and why she had chosen to come to the top of the mountains on our island. But there was no way to ask. Instead we chatted in class about words and writers, and the other girls and I listened to Miss O'Hare reading our stories, amused that her accent had become just like ours.

I liked Miss O'Hare's class, but for Maths and Science, I spent my time staring out the window, across the hills, wondering how long it would take me to get back to Kingston. Mr. Robinson, a short, stout, square-faced man with greying hair, didn't seem to notice my inattention. When he wasn't writing things on the board, with his back to us, he talked on and on in a drone, looking over our heads. He didn't seem to think we were capable of learning what he was teaching.

One girl in the class, Venetia Tucker, became my best friend. When you moved here, Dulcinea, you reminded me so much of her: the way you walked, shook your hair; the way you laughed. Venetia was always telling jokes, was always ready with a sharp pin to pop pretences and pomposity. One of her favourite targets was Mr. Robinson, who taught us to be scientific and pious at the same time.

In one class he lectured that people were descended from apes, and in another he said that God created Adam and Eve. In one lesson he said that our island had lain in the sea for millions of years before the Blue Mountains slowly rose from the depths; and in another he recited that God had created heaven and earth in seven days. Mr. Robinson regurgitated whatever was appropriate for the particular class, what the educational authorities decreed.

"Sir, maybe God created two apes named Adam and Eve, and then human beings descended from them," Venetia said one day. "These apes probably looked at their babies and thought that they were as ugly as sin, so they banished them from the Garden of Eden."

But Mr. Robinson had no sense of humour, and he told Venetia he was going to have a word with her parents as soon as he could. Venetia, however, was not deterred.

"Sir, if we can pray for people who do evil," she said in the religion class, "couldn't we pray for Satan so he can change his ways? Then we could all live happily ever after."

Mr. Robinson stared at her then lifted his gaze above our heads, as usual, focusing on the pale green wall at the back of the classroom. "There are some things we cannot pray for. Satan is a lost cause."

"But –" and Venetia continued her argument, while our classmates giggled, and I looked out the window, listening.

Venetia often remarked that it must take at least two jobs to be rich, and that's why Mr. Robinson was both a pastor and a teacher: he needed the income from both professions to keep up his lifestyle. The car he drove up the hill to our school was so big that he could barely see above the steering wheel, and we'd heard from other students who'd visited Montego Bay that he had a huge house in the town. You know, I've always disliked people who like to live in mansions, Dulcinea.

Sometimes Venetia would come home with me for an hour or so, because Granny knew her parents and, in fact, had delivered her at birth.

"From the moment this child came out of her mother's womb, her mouth never stop moving," Granny laughed. "What a little mouthamassy you are, Venetia." And Venetia grinned, never taking offence.

She talked for both of us, and she knew everybody's business. If Venetia didn't have the gift of sight, she had the gift of surmise, speculation, and great imagination. She told me that Miss O'Hare was supposed to have got married in her homeland, but that the bridegroom hadn't shown up at the church on the wedding day; she described what Miss O'Hare had been wearing, the weeping of her relatives, and how Miss O'Hare had fled across the ocean to the farthest place she could find – the District of Look Behind. I knew that Venetia was destined for a life on the stage, in pantomime and later in politics, but I preferred as always to keep my visions to myself.

At three o'clock each day, when school was dismissed, I walked back up the dirt track to Granny's house, and that's when the real lessons began, Dulcinea. Every afternoon, before the daily drizzle or downpour, Granny took me for a walk through the bush, to gather herbs, flowers, bark. I had to be careful as I walked because these limestone hills hid deep sinkholes; if you stepped on a layer of limestone that was too thin, you could plunge through to oblivion. No one knew how deep the holes were, but Granny was as sure-footed as a goat, and she taught me to follow in her steps. The Cockpit Country was full of caves and hollows where strange plants grew and where hundreds of bats lived, and Uncle had told me to watch out for snakes and scorpions, but Granny herself trod fearlessly. Everything had a use, she said, and I realized where my mother had got that from. Don't chop down the mango tree, she had told my father. Even if it doesn't give us fruit, it will provide shade.

Granny had never been to a doctor in her life, and the people who lived in the villages around us preferred to make the trek to our house rather than go to the doctor in Accompong, the main town in the District of Look Behind. That's where the famous Maroon peace treaty had been signed, and where Uncle Selwyn lived. I saw few of Granny's clients because they visited when I was at school, but every evening I helped Granny prepare for them. We spread our harvest on the dining table, and she showed me how to chop things up and place them in jars, covered with oil. Other things we left out to dry before boiling and bottling them.

"When you have cramps and I give you ginger-tea to drink, what do you think stop the pain?" Granny asked me once. "The ginger or because you believe the tea helping you?"

"The ginger," I replied, and I was surprised when Granny laughed.

"Everybody who come to this house believe I can help them in some way," she told me. "I could give them anything at all and it would probably work. But I always give them the right thing. Remember that."

I nodded but I wasn't inclined to remember any of this. I had my own preoccupations.

"Granny, can you see things?" I asked her. She looked at me for a long time before answering.

"Not in the way you can. That's your gift, passed down from your great-grandfather."

"I don't want it."

Granny smiled. "Sweetheart, is God decide."

God decided that I would live with my grandmother for ten years, Dulcinea, and as the time went by, I gradually forgot

94

about going back to Kingston. I saw Mama and Annette every Christmas anyway, when they came to the Cockpit Country to spend time with us in the District of Look Behind. Granny would start stewing the fruit for our Christmas pudding from the beginning of November, and she also bought a goat and chickens to fatten for the never-ending Christmas celebration. We started eating on Christmas Eve and didn't stop until New Year's Day. Granny invited Miss O'Hare to join us as well because, as Granny said, "she doesn't have a soul up here". Miss O'Hare soon became a part of our family, in every sense of the word.

Annette seemed more beautiful each time I saw her, and I felt a strange pride that she was my sister, pride mixed with a small amount of envy that was easily squashed. It was easy to love Annette because her niceness was a part of her beauty. I'd never heard her say an unkind word about anyone. When she came up to the hills, she immediately tried to help with whatever Granny and I had to do. Granny remarked that Annette looked more and more like my father, while I took after my mother's side of the family.

After New Year, Annette and Mama stayed with us for the next big celebration in the hills, when we all descended on Accompong for the Maroon Festival on January 6, to celebrate, yes, the signing of the peace treaty back in 1739. You would have loved it, Dulcinea – dancing and laughing and non-stop eating and drum-beating. And throughout it all, someone would keep blowing the abeng, and you could hear the echoes of the horn coming back at us over the mountains. Granny told me that, a long time ago, this cow horn was the only way the Maroons could communicate with one another across the hills, and the haunting sound would strike terror into the hearts of any soldiers out on patrol.

Before she journeyed back to the other side of the world, from whence she'd come, Miss O'Hare never missed a festival. She said that the dances were like those in Ireland, and she would jump right in, kicking up her legs and clapping her hands as we pranced under the Kindah tree – this old mango tree where Maroon leader Cudjoe and Granny's ancestors had gathered to plot ways to fight the enemy. Did trees live that long? I asked Granny. This one does, she replied.

Miss O'Hare danced with wild abandon, apparently determined to shake off the sadness that dogged her. Sometimes she looked like a child having an epileptic fit, but I kept that thought to myself. At my second festival in the Cockpit Country, when I was fifteen, I noticed that my Uncle Selwyn's eyes followed Miss O'Hare's every movement, and a sudden vision of him bundled up in more clothes than anyone should wear made me shiver in the fading evening sun. They would both soon be leaving us. Even up here, at the top of these jagged hills, life played out its little comedies.

After the days of celebrating and being with my sister, it took me a long time to get back to "normal" when Annette and Mama returned to Kingston, driven down the mountainside in Uncle Selwyn's Morris Oxford, as they had been driven up.

My time with Granny was also framed by hurricanes, and that's how I remember everything, Dulcinea. The year that I turned fifteen was also the year Hurricane Flora blew off the roof of our house and nearly wiped out Uncle Selwyn's coffee farm. Before the winds hit, I insisted that we had to leave the house, because I couldn't get rid of the feeling of something bad about to happen, and Granny listened to me. We threw a few pieces of clothes into a canvas bag and rushed down the dirt track, even as the rain began to fall. For the next three days, Granny and I huddled with Uncle in his house in Accompong. The house was built of brick, and sheltered from the direct winds by the curve of the hillside. The rain came down by the bucketfuls, and the wind was like a woman gone off her head, screaming and slapping at everything in her path. During a lull on the second day, Uncle went out to check if Miss O'Hare was safe in her dormitory at the school, and he came back hours later covered from head to foot in mud. The rain had turned the hills into a bog, he said, but Miss O'Hare was fine. Hurricane Flora wasn't finished with us, however, and the rain kept coming, threatening to flush us down into the valleys.

When it was all over, even Uncle Selwyn cried at the devastation, but we got word from Kingston that things in the east of the island were far worse, with bridges down, rivers flooded, and houses washed away. We worried about Mama and Annette, but in the meantime there was work to be done. Nearly everyone in the District of Look Behind had suffered some damage, and we all tried to help one another. We washed, scrubbed, swept, painted and re-planted, and eventually regained our sense of order. As soon as he could, Uncle Selwyn drove to Kingston to check on Mama and Annette, and he was gone for four dread-filled days. But he reported back that they were fine, although the house on Upper Wellington was leaking from a hundred cracks in the ceilings. Uncle said he had fixed the roof and cleaned up the yard, where everything, except the old mango tree, had been uprooted once more.

When we could finally stop talking about Hurricane Flora, and when Uncle Selwyn's farm started bouncing back, he told Granny he was going to propose to Miss O'Hare. He brought her up to the house the following Saturday. She was shining as if someone had lit a candle behind her eyes.

They were to be married the following year, after my sixteenth birthday, and Annette, Venetia and I were to be bridesmaids. But Cleo intervened. Two days before the wedding in August, Hurricane Cleo dumped tubs of water on the mountain and swamped Uncle Selwyn's farm once more. They had to postpone the ceremony until mid-December and so, that year, our celebrations stretched from the wedding through Christmas until the peace-treaty festival. Venetia commented that I was getting fat from all the eating, but I became lean again with the work we had to do when Hurricane Inez, "the crazy one", passed through. She battered the hills before moving on to pound Cuba and later Mexico, killing more than one thousand people in her murderous fury.

By then I was seventeen and had graduated from school, with thoughts of moving back to Kingston to find work. But Inez bashed those ideas. After the destruction she'd wrought, Uncle Selwyn decided he'd had enough. He sold the coffee farm, rented out his house, and he and Miss O'Hare (which is what I still called her because "Auntie" sounded strange) packed up and booked their flight on BOAC. Miss O'Hare had got a job teaching at a school in London and Uncle was going to search for any employment that was suitable. Miss O'Hare left me all her books, while Uncle told Granny to use whatever she needed from the rent she would collect from his house. The rest of the money would go in the bank.

One of Uncle's neighbours had bought his car and this man drove us all to Palisadoes Airport in Kingston, where we met up with Mama and Annette. It was the first time I'd been to the airport, and the first time that I saw a plane sitting quietly on land. We chatted and exchanged hugs, and when Uncle and Miss O'Hare finally had to go inside the departure hall, Granny, Mama, Annette and I trod upstairs to the airport's gallery for a last sight of them. We waved and waved as they crossed the distance from the building to the BOAC plane, the wind causing Uncle to hold on to the front of his jacket, and causing Miss O'Hare's black curls to whip about her face. I cried to see them go, knowing there was no way to tell them that they'd be better off staying on the island, hurricane or no hurricane. Their departure meant that if I, too, left the District of Look Behind, Granny would be alone. So I said goodbye to Kingston for the second time and journeyed back to the hills with her. Two days later, Venetia travelled in the opposite direction, saying goodbye to us and heading to "town" and to her career as an actress. The mountains felt lonely without her laughter.

During the next three years, Granny and I barricaded ourselves against several more storms or watched from afar as they tore through the land. They all had women's names: Beulah, Gladys, Alma. But it was a hurricane with a man's name that had the greatest impact on our lives: Hurricane Francis. That's what Granny called him, Dulcinea: "Hurricane Francis". Yes, Francis McKnight, Cheryl's father and – I know you guessed – Trevor's father too.

I saw him for the first time when he swept into the Cockpit Country to sell insurance, going from house to house and charmingly instilling dread about what might happen with the next blast of wind and rain. He arrived at Granny's house at lunchtime on a Tuesday, just as we had sat down at the table, and Granny invited him in and set another plate when he'd stated his business. He was dressed in a long-sleeved white shirt, black pants and blue tie, and he carried a leather briefcase. He didn't look much older than I was, but he seemed to have come from a different world.

"The next hurricane might be much worse," he told Granny, sipping his fruit punch and glancing in my direction. "We haven't really seen anything yet. We are due for a really big one which will make everything in the last few years look like a little drizzle."

"You don't say," Granny remarked.

"Yes, in this day and age, everybody needs insurance. So many things can happen."

"Well, I don't disagree with that," Granny said, nodding solemnly.

Francis talked on, and I listened closely, liking the sound of his voice, which had a husky, caressing quality. It was the kind of voice that cigarette smoking had given my father before destroying his lungs.

"Haven't you suffered a lot of damage with the recent hurricanes?" Francis asked. "Wouldn't you like some help when you have to rebuild?"

"Oh, the roof has blown off a couple of times," Granny said airily, shaking her thick grey plaits. "I think I've seen more hurricanes in my time than the number of years you've been on this earth. And I'm still here."

Francis guffawed, as if she'd just said something immensely funny, and he quickly launched into more reasons why insurance was a good idea. I could've told him to stop wasting his breath; Granny wasn't about to plunk down money for something as intangible as what he was trying to sell. In the District of Look Behind, insurance was your neighbour's willingness to help when times were bad.

Our visitor finished his lunch, thanked us, and told us to think about everything. He announced that he would be back to talk to us, and he waved a friendly goodbye as he got into his small car. Granny said she hoped his tyres would survive the potholes on his way down the hill, and we both went back inside the house to clean up. I didn't expect to see him again.

He was back two weeks later, again at lunchtime, and the procedure from the first visit was repeated, with Granny now saying: "You could talk till you blue in the face. Me not buying any insurance." When he laughed, she added, "But I don't suppose that will stop you from coming up here."

Francis told us that he worked for a company named Mutual Building Society which had been around for nearly a hundred years. The founders in the 19th century had had a vision to assist "all poor people to become proud home-owners" and now they were branching into insurance because it was no good having a roof over your head if hurricanes blew it off every year and you couldn't manage to replace it.

"You're probably right about that, but I never had a problem replacing mine," Granny said proudly.

Francis tried to explain the advantages of using insurance money rather than one's own for such repairs, but Granny just smiled at him in her mysterious fashion.

"Boy, your old lady really stubborn," he said to me later, when I walked with him to his car. "Everything just go in one ear and out the next."

"Yes, she has a mind of her own," I agreed.

Francis kept coming up to the hills, saying he wouldn't stop until he convinced Granny of the benefits of insurance, especially before the next hurricane pounded us. But by the fourth visit, I knew that he was really coming to see me, and it made me smile as Miss O'Hare had done years before, when she noticed Uncle Selwyn watching her.

After each lunch, Francis and I would go for a stroll through the district, and I pointed out plants, birds and butterflies; we had what must have been the biggest butterfly in the world, right up there in the Cockpit Country, its yellow-and-black wings wider than my open hand. Francis was interested in everything, and as I showed him around, I realized how much the hills had become home to me – I loved them but I still yearned to leave.

Before Francis, I had half-accepted the future Granny had mapped out for me, but now I began dreaming of an escape. I didn't want to be a medicine-woman; I didn't want to tell people to put their affairs in order because they might not be around in a week's time; and I didn't want to spend hours brooding over stomach-twisting visions, trying to decipher their dark meanings. Francis was going to be a way out. And, if there were herbs in the hills to help me, I would use them. But Granny refused to cooperate.

"I can't tell you what to do with your life," she said. "But remember this: when the hurricane has done its damage, it moves on, with not a look behind. And nothing you do will make any difference."

Unlike Granny, though, I believed in insurance. I brewed certain teas for myself and for Francis, trusting the herbs to ward off bad luck and to keep us together. All of our walks now ended with our stripping off each other's clothes and coming together amidst the plants and trees. We made love like my ancestors might have done, with my back against a tree, my legs wrapped around his hips, he leaning into me as he held me up. The first time there was pain, like the cramps for which Granny used to make me ginger tea, but afterwards it seemed as if even the hills were happy, welcoming us with flowers and birdsong.

Twenty-five visits – I counted them – after he first came to Granny's house, Francis finally proposed when I told him I was thinking of moving to England to live with my uncle and aunt-in-law. I wanted to go there to study, I said, maybe to become a schoolteacher.

"Why would you want to do that, Mavis, when we're going to get married very soon?" he asked.

"We are?"

"Of course."

When I told Granny about it, she shook her head and said, "Just remember you always have a home here."

I was angry that she wasn't more enthusiastic about my impending marriage, and about Francis, but these feelings didn't last long because freedom was mine. I spent the next two weeks humming to myself as I prepared to go back to Kingston to organize my wedding with Mama and Annette, who hadn't yet met Francis. Granny said she would come later, and I was hoping that she would decide to stay and live on Upper Wellington Road where I could still see her when I wanted.

Francis came to fetch me late on a Sunday morning, when the mist hadn't yet cleared from the hills, and the sun came through in smoky slants of light. As he put my suitcase in the trunk of the car, Granny hugged me for a long time, under the flame of the forest tree, and she rubbed my back as if I were still a child. Both our faces were wet from tears, but I knew I had to leave.

The silence of the Cockpit Country filled the car as we drove down the rutted, winding road until we reached an area where we could pick up one of the two radio stations, and Francis turned the music on.

We got to Upper Wellington Road just as it was getting dark, and my mother and sister seemed overjoyed to see me. It was like Christmastime. Mama had prepared dinner for us, and Francis beamed as they made him welcome. But that evening, Dulcinea, I could not eat because I saw that Francis's eyes seemed glued to Annette's every gesture. He tried to hide it, looking sideways when she got up to go to the kitchen, or when she shifted in her chair, but I noticed. He even seemed to blush when she spoke directly to him, the blood rising underneath his cinnamon skin.

It was the same the next day, and the day after that, even as Mama, Annette and I chatted with him about the wedding and made plans. We were supposed to be married in six weeks and, during that whole time, Francis and Annette circled around each other like two mating peeny-wallies, their light flickering in the darkness. I wanted to scream at them to stop, but there was nothing I could do except to withdraw into myself, and try to ignore this particular vision. I couldn't talk to Mama; I was the one she had sent away to the hills, not Annette. So, I watched, waiting for Francis to come to his senses or for Annette's goodness to assert itself.

Granny arrived, with all the ingredients for the wedding cake, and she saw my sadness and silent rage. "Don't worry," she said. "Everything will be all right." But she wasn't the one with the gift of sight. Three days before our wedding, I knew what I would find when I got up in the middle of the night and walked into Annette's room.

They were both apologetic, Dulcinea, and Annette begged me to forgive her, but there were no words for what I felt. If I could have killed them both, I would have. I attacked Annette, wailing and slapping her face, and it took three of them – Francis, Mama and Granny – to pull me away. I ran outside in the darkness and flung myself down under the old mango tree, and I bawled, Dulcinea, loud enough to wake up the whole neighbourhood, like a dog howling in pain.

The next day I fled to the Cockpit Country with Granny, leaving my sister and my fiancé to cancel the wedding. I yearned for Francis to come after me, but it was a futile wish. Then, on a day when there were no more tears, Granny placed a white enamel mug in front of me, and said: "If you *don't* want to keep it, drink this." I looked at the light golden liquid, with the leaves at the bottom, and was tempted to drink it and cleanse myself of Francis's seed, but, in the end, I pushed the mug away.

Trevor was born in the District of Look Behind, Dulcinea, in the week that a tropical storm named Gilda sent mud sliding down the hills to the sea. He was born four months after my sister and Francis got married in a lavish ceremony to which neither Granny nor I was invited, and in the year that our new prime minister kept promising that "better must come". Granny kept repeating those words to me, too, as if I didn't know what the future held, despite all the political slogans on the radio and the false sense of optimism that was filling the land, reaching even to the Cockpit Country, where we governed ourselves.

My grandmother was the one who delivered Trevor, who held him up for me to look at, pronouncing that he, too, had the mountains in him. He was beautiful to look at, and Granny's face held a glow whenever she took him in her arms.

"I never knew I would live to see great-grandchildren," she said. "What a blessing. What a blessing."

For the next two years there was no Christmas family reunion, but we got news of the happenings in Kingston, from relatives and friends of relatives who passed through to visit or to consult with Granny. Interspersed with the news of political shootings and killings, we heard that Annette had also given birth, to a girl.

Her daughter, Cheryl, was born in the year that our beloved prime minister announced we were now a Socialist country, and in the month that Hurricane Carmen soaked Kingston and the rest of the south coast in rain. But this time the Cockpit Country stayed dry, except for the afternoon drizzles. While Annette was miles away, probably nursing her daughter through the floods, Granny and I watched and clapped as Trevor learned to walk, tottering around the wide yard.

Even with the joy Trevor brought, anger still gnawed at my insides, Dulcinea, and I envisioned all kinds of calamities for those two who had hurt me so much. But I would never have wished for what happened to Annette. This was one of the times when my sight failed me, or perhaps I just chose not to see, preferred not to know.

To celebrate their second wedding anniversary, Annette and Francis left Cheryl with Mama one evening and went to see a movie called "Car Wash". The government had declared a state of emergency that January, but no one quite realized yet how vicious the political gangs would become. As Annette and Francis left Castle Theatre, with plans to go for dinner, they heard gunshots and saw people scampering like frightened goats, screaming in panic. With bullets flying left and right, my sister and everyone else emerging from the theatre raced blindly for cover. Some tried to go back inside the building but the people coming out didn't know what was happening. Pushing and shoving ensued, with no one going in either direction. Annette and Francis sprinted instead for the nearby police station, and they ran straight into the gun battle. We found out later that several gunmen had attacked the police station, killing one policeman. As the gunmen tried to escape, the remaining seven officers opened fire, turning respectable Cross Roads into the Wild West. A bullet hit Annette in the shoulder, and another lodged in her spine. Francis covered her body with his, screaming for help as more bullets whizzed above them. When all finally grew quiet, a few people came over to help Francis carry Annette to his car, and he drove like a madman to St. Andrews Hospital.

Late that night, Granny and I got word from Mama that Annette was still hanging on, waiting for us to arrive. The doctors had managed to remove the bullet from her shoulder, but they could do nothing about the one embedded in her backbone. Mama was hoping that Granny's bush medicine could provide a miracle, but it was too late even for that. After a sleepless night, Granny and I made the journey to Kingston, heading down the hillside before sunrise, with Trevor sitting on my lap in the back seat of a ramshackle taxi. But I knew before we got to the hospital that this would be the last time I would see my sister. I sat beside her bed during the final hours, listening to her rasping words as she asked me to take care of Cheryl, and watching her spirit depart as I'd watched my father's. Through it all, Francis wept like a fool, and I might have felt sorry for him had my own pain been less.

Uncle Selwyn and Miss O'Hare came home for Annette's funeral, leaving a bitingly cold winter behind in England. They each had lost several shades of colour, from the lack of sunshine, and they were exhausted by the long flight. Uncle Selwyn didn't recognize the country he had left ten years before and couldn't understand the violence he'd read about in the newspapers abroad.

On nine-night, before Annette's church ceremony, we all sat on the verandah at Upper Wellington Road, talking, crying, laughing and trying to stifle the anger. We'd learned from *The Star* that Annette was only one of the 150 people killed so far that year in the violence, but the figures didn't make us feel any better. And I knew that no one would end up in the General Penitentiary for the bullets that took her. At the wake, Cheryl and Trevor played together, not quite sure what was wrong with the big people, and the neighbours trooped in and out, drinking rum and eating the fried fish Mama and Granny had prepared. Through it all, Francis kept repeating, like a stuck 78 record, the details of what had happened and how he wished he'd been the one now lying in the funeral parlour.

Both Uncle Selwyn and Miss O'Hare drank too much rum, and their tales of living abroad came pouring out. I heard parts of their conversation as if from far away, as I sat in a corner of the verandah with my eyes closed.

"I never knew that place would be so cold and the people so unfriendly," Uncle Selwyn said. "You know, the people I work with during the day pretend to smile at me, but when I pass them on the street in the evening or on the weekends, they'll walk right by, as if they don't know me from Adam."

"Yes," Miss O'Hare pitched in, "As if it would kill them to say hello. And you wouldn't believe how much trouble we had trying to find a place to live. If Selwyn went by himself to look at a place, it suddenly was no longer up for rent. But I would go to the same place later, and they would be willing to rent it to me, until they heard the word 'Ireland'."

"You should come back home," someone on the verandah said.

"To what?" Uncle asked. "Look at all this violence taking place here now. Is what happen?"

But no one could answer him because everyone was in shock. Over the past two years we had all learned new words: Democratic Socialism, State of Emergency, Gun Court, Coup. And people joked that coup must mean chicken coop because no one could've imagined the fast descent into madness.

Through all the talk, Granny kept muttering: "It not right. It just not right, for someone so young to die."

Trevor, Cheryl and you, Dulcinea, grew up with violence always there in the background, and you got used to it. But that year was just the start for us. We kept hearing on the radio that "better must come, better must come one day" because someone had recorded a song with these words, in praise of the prime minister. But even as the words bounced around in our heads, we all knew better.

After Annette's funeral, Uncle Selwyn and Miss O'Hare went back to the cold, and Mama followed them a few months later, selling the house on Upper Wellington Road. She gave Granny and me half of the money, and said she hoped that I would come with Trevor and Cheryl to join her in Birmingham, but I knew I wouldn't be going anywhere. Instead, I moved into Francis' house to be a mother to Cheryl, because, as Granny said, God decided it so.

Granny herself died four years later, in her sleep up in the hills, a few days before Christmas. That year we had gone from Democratic Socialism to Social Democracy, and watched as hundreds were gunned down all over the island; and we'd also had to barricade ourselves against other storms. Four months earlier, Hurricane Allen had torn along the north coast, flooding the parishes and blowing off roofs, including Granny's. She had had enough, seen enough. "I'm tired, Mavis," she had told me, the last time we spoke.

I left the children with Francis and travelled alone to the Cockpit Country, watching over Granny's body as I waited for my mother and uncle to arrive. We buried her up there in the District of Look Behind, filled with memories of long-ago family reunions. Afterwards, it was back to England for Mama and Uncle Selwyn, never to return.

Through all these years of being in Francis's house, I've never said anything about Trevor's father, and Francis never once asked: "Is he mine? Is Trevor mine?" probably because he already knew the answer. How can you forgive a man like that? It's as if for him our time in the hills never happened, as if I imagined it all.

When he moved into that woman's mansion, and Cheryl decided to stay with me and Trevor, I felt a kind of peace, Dulcinea. Without knowing anything, Cheryl had chosen us, making up for all the betrayals. But then she and Trevor got themselves in a certain situation, creeping around and behaving like creatures of the night. Did she ever tell you what went on, Dulcinea, you who loved her so much? I tried to be blind, deaf and dumb, but I know it's mostly my fault, and my heart hurts for us all. How do you put all this on a canvas – all the silences, all the misunderstandings, all the tears cried in the dark?

I'll have to tell them everything, Dulcinea. They'll have to know the truth because this can't go on. We'll each have to choose our path now, like you did.

CHAPTER NINE

CHERYL

New York

Josh is standing in front of Grant's Tomb when I arrive at Riverside Park shortly before nine in the morning. I was afraid that he wouldn't show up, but he is here, looking older and thinner, with his greying hair in need of a trim.

We gaze at each other awkwardly for a long moment and then hug, tightly, somewhat clumsily, in the shadow of the mausoleum. I feel my breasts pressing uncomfortably against his chest as his body trembles, and I pull back, embarrassed, knowing that you are watching us, with your eloquent eyes and taunting smile.

"Thanks for coming," I say, looking in his eyes.

He meets my look then glances away. "Yeah, I only decided at the last moment. But I wanted to say goodbye, to try to move on, finally."

I nod, in sympathy, and we both stand there staring at the river and listening to the squeals of children being pushed by their nannies on nearby swings.

"I met her for the first time just down the road," Josh says softly. "She was on her way to the gallery."

"Yes, I know. She told me about it. Paul is coming, too, before he goes to open the gallery. He said he might be slightly late."

"And Susie from *The Times* should be here anytime now. She wants to write an article. I hope you don't mind?"

I shrug. I already know what kind of story she's going to write, Dulci: overheated fiction, without a clue to the real you.

"What happened in the last days?" Josh asks, and I wonder whether to tell him the truth.

"She decided to go, and I helped."

"How? Was it really cancer?"

I take a deep breath, feeling the familiar heaviness in my chest and head. My words come out hesitantly at first, then in a stream. I need this relief of telling someone about what happened, but I also know that Josh doesn't deserve the burden of hearing everything. I describe to him how you went, how you planned it all. I tell him that you were ready, that your work was done, but I don't say a word about us. He has had enough pain.

When I am finished, Josh stays silent for several seconds. "That's just like her," he says finally. "It had to be her way."

"Yes. Look, Paul is coming."

We watch as Paul approaches, walking briskly across the pavement.

He kisses me on both cheeks and shakes Josh's hand.

"Well, this is a fitting meeting point," he laughs. "Grant's Tomb. Final resting place of the great Ulysses S., general and 18th president."

"Trust you to know your history," Josh remarks.

"I have nothing better to do while I sit and wait for someone to enter the gallery and buy a painting," Paul jokes. "My days are long and empty."

"Poor you," I say, and we all laugh. When we stop, we are not quite sure what to say any more.

"I really miss, Cinea," Paul declares, his face serious. "I've lost too many friends over the years, and it gets harder every time."

All the usual drivel about "gone to a better place", "let's

remember her as she was", and "she lives on in our hearts" goes through my head, Dulci. That's what I heard our neighbours murmuring to your parents at the funeral, and though it was meant to comfort, it doesn't mean a thing. But before I can stop myself, I find myself blurting out, "I think about her all the time."

"Me, too," Josh says, in a reluctant admission.

The silence returns, and I am grateful when Susie from *The Times* announces her presence with: "It's bloody warm this morning, isn't it?" And, without waiting for an answer: "Right, what's happening with the ashes? I have a 3 o'clock deadline."

★   ★   ★

This is the article she has written, Dulci. It's bound to make you laugh. I don't recall the breeze or seeing any birds, but perhaps I was thinking of other things.

Ashes in the Wind: An Artist Returns Home
By Susie Thomas

New York: Caribbean artist Cinea Verse returned yesterday to the city she loved, when her best friend, her husband, and her agent gathered in Riverside Park, Manhattan, to scatter her ashes in the warm wind blowing above the Hudson River.

Verse, who died four weeks ago after battling an undisclosed illness, was a young diva of the art world, known for her personal style as well as for her huge canvases filled with the colors of the Caribbean. During the more than 10 years that she lived in New York, her work was snapped up by wealthy collectors, and she even appeared on television to discuss art with such personalities as Oprah.

In an interview, at the height of her fame, Verse

told me that she really had no influences; that her work was inspired by her homeland, where a kind of madness reigned. Her vibrant reds, oranges and blues were a reflection of the place where she had grown up, she said, and her work depicted scenes that stuck in her mind: a green and black hummingbird drinking from a red hibiscus flower or a young woman all dressed up for a party in a blazing scarlet dress, her hair in long artificial braids. These images were made all the more striking by the size of her canvases, which were usually taller than Verse herself.

Cinea Verse was born Dulcinea Gertrude Evers in Kingston, Jamaica, to a builder father and a home-maker mother. She attended a Catholic high school, where she astounded her teachers with her artistic skills. One instructor, Fitzroy Walcott, said in a telephone interview: "Verse had an eye for detail not common among her peers. She could draw anything and make you look and look again."

After graduation from high school, Verse worked at a bank but was fired when she got into a fight with a client who had insulted her. Details about the incident are sketchy, but the altercation resulted in Verse losing her clothing in public. As she was a beautiful woman, and not at all shy, one can only imagine the attention this must have garnered.

Soon after this episode, Verse began painting seriously. She left home and went to live in a friend's dorm room at one of the local universities. She credited this friend, Cheryl McKnight, with provid-ing the support necessary to pursue her dream of becoming an artist. Verse earned money by selling her work to professors on campus or, cheaply, to friends. McKnight owns some of these early pieces, which are now in great demand.

Verse arrived in New York in the Nineties to take part in a group show, and she immediately decided that this was the city for her. Paul Grimes, owner of the Guacha Gallery on Broadway, who at the time specialized in Latin American art, was one of the first people in the business to notice Verse's work, and he subsequently became her sole agent. He filled his gallery with her canvases, the bold colors enticing unwary clients. He also held much-publicized openings where guests listened to reggae music, ate jerk-chicken off arty earthenware, and drank rum-punch from oversized glasses. Whether in a drunken stupor or in the grip of admiration, people bought the paintings, and Verse was on her way to art stardom.

Along the way, she married and separated from art historian Josh Scarbinsky, although they never divorced. Scarbinsky was there in Riverside Park yesterday to help free her ashes, in a poignant good-bye. After the split, Verse was linked to several others – famous and not-so-famous – as her love of socializing seemed to feed her work, much as Picasso needed sensual stimulus for his art.

But is it fair to mention Verse and Picasso in the same breath? Critics have not yet decided on Verse's place in the pantheon of artists, and in this age of too much art and too little talent, it would be easy to say that Verse exemplified the commoditization of culture so apparent nowadays. Indeed, her story has played out before: a gifted young artist hits New York, is befriended by important people and, before anyone can blink, the work is a must-have for every banker's wall.

But Cinea Verse was, is different. You cannot look at her paintings without being drawn into a world that at first seems bright and cheerful but later is revealed to have disturbing and forlorn undertones. As Ovid said, "art lies in concealing art", and Verse was a mistress of this. She painted everyday subjects, but their appeal will endure mainly because of her undeniable artistry, her eye for looking beyond the obvious. Stand in front of any one of her canvases, and you will find your attention being held, as apparent simplicity turns into complexity, commanding you to look beyond the dazzling hues of Verse's islandscape.

Her friend McKnight said that Verse (whom she still calls Dulcinea) found "freedom" in New York and was able to develop as the artist she was meant to be. Her unacknowledged nostalgia for an island to which she never intended to return also fed her creativity.

"Dulci saw things in a way few people do," McKnight said. "And she waited for you to see them as well. Once you've seen, you can never go back to what you were."

Before she died, Verse asked McKnight to bring half of her ashes back to New York, following the funeral services in her homeland. McKnight fulfilled that request in moving fashion yesterday when she, Scarbinsky and Grimes released Verse's remains to the winds that swayed the trees in Riverside Park and lifted the leaves around Grant's Tomb. We all watched in awe as two white sea gulls circled overhead while the ashes settled gracefully on the waters of the Hudson, flowing to Lower New York Bay and on to the Atlantic Ocean. It was a scene with the beauty of art.

CHAPTER TEN

MARJORIE EVERS

Hibiscus Drive, Kingston

When I was in school, Sweetheart, the teachers used to embarrass me every single day, calling on me to recite things that I could never remember. Who needs to have their head full of all that rubbish? Who cares when the Spaniard discovered the island? Or when Emancipation took place? I was never brave enough to ask: Do I look emancipated to you? But I wish I had been.

The other children used to snigger as I stood there staring blankly into space, and I squirmed when they exchanged whispers of "dunce-bat". Even if I wasn't smart and didn't want to be, I still had feelings. At first, I hated them all, but, after a while, their words no longer had any effect. None whatsoever. It was as if they weren't even there. You inherited that from me, you know – this ability, heaven-sent, to shrug off spite and stupidity. When I look in the mirror, I see your eyes looking back at me. Eyes with that light in them that so few people understood. No one was ever going to control or confine you. When I graduated from school, I tore up all those report cards with the proclamations of: *Needs to learn to pay attention, daydreams too much, unable to concentrate* – proclamations that made my father rant to my mother in frustration.

You see, Sweetheart, my father was a wordsmith, a man who could recite poetry by heart. From Wordsworth to

Miss Lou, he knew every rhyme written by God knows who. The people who read my father's articles in *The Gleaner* were convinced that he was the smartest man on the island, and they wrote letters to tell him so and to urge him to get involved in politics, even to run for Prime Minister. These letters were his pride and joy. And I was his shame. Every evening he sat me down in front of books and made me utter words aloud like a parrot, words which I forgot as soon as they left my mouth. And every morning he had the same instruction: *Try not to make a fool of yourself at school today. I'm tired of having to go and talk to the teachers.* Yes, Papa, I smiled, ignoring the everlasting look of disappointment on his face. My mother would try to stick up for me by saying: the child is doing her best, Nate. His reply was always the same. *Is her best to be last in her class every year?*

My father, Nathan Henriques, had a tradition to uphold and he saw it all slipping away with me, his only child. From the time I could listen, or maybe it was from the moment of my birth, my father filled my head with stories of his great-great-grand-somebody who had helped to start the first newspaper in the Caribbean. And the ancestors of his great-great-grand-somebody who had fled from Portugal or Spain because of persecution and, after arriving with not a thing, had turned themselves into merchants and builders, kings on the island. Those were his words, Sweetheart. My father was like most light-skinned people back then, always proud of the lighter half in their blood. "And what about the African side, Papa?" I asked when everyone started sporting dreadlocks. But he had no stories about that, apart from what I myself learned in school. Enslavement. Abolition. Emancipation. No kings of any kind.

He passed the synagogue on Duke Street every day as he went to work at the newspaper, and although he never set foot inside, for him it was the most beautiful building in Kingston, with its gleaming white paint and wide windows.

Another ancestral relative had helped with the construction, Papa informed me more times than I could count. But the synagogue was something your own father might have built, Sweetheart.

Yes, they liked each other, my father and yours – two short, brainy, light-skinned men who loved to talk about buildings. And politics. And history. And poetry. I met your father, Sweetheart, when he came to oversee work on our house, replacing the roof which the last hurricane had just about taken off. My father was impressed by your father's knowledge, and pleased that he knew everything that had ever been written in the newspaper. He kept inviting him to the house after the work was finished, and before I knew it, I was walking down the aisle in white. The aisle of Holy Trinity Cathedral, where my mother always went, not the synagogue on Duke Street. After that shining moment, I was pregnant all the time, and whatever little energy I'd had for thinking soon went into raising you and your brothers.

But now, all I can do is think. And dream.

I've been sleeping mostly in your old room, Sweetheart, because whenever I sleep beside your father, I get strange visions of waking up in the night and going to the kitchen for the ice-pick, or for the bread knife with the long serrated blade. I'm doing my best, though, to control myself, and not give in to the rage.

Why didn't you tell me you were sick? All those times when you called long-distance, you never said a word. If you coughed and I asked about it, you said it was just a bit of the flu because America was cold. I could have come to New York and cared for you, despite my fear of being up there in a plane where no human being really belongs. I would've taken a boat, swum, anything, if only you'd said something.

Now ever since your friend called with the news that you'd gone, I've been having the same dream. In it, I stand watching you walk along the thin ledge of a high white wall, stepping proudly like a cat. But as I watch with growing fear, you suddenly lose your balance and plunge headfirst. With my heart in my mouth, I race towards you, but I know I won't be in time to prevent your fall. Then I wake up

I tell my dream to your friend's mother-auntie, and she nods and says she gets dreams about you, too. She doesn't say much when I go down to talk with her on her verandah. She lets me pour my heart out, and she just sits there bobbing her head, while her dogs lie in the shade of the sweetsop tree. The tree is full of fruit now, and I have a clear image of you and your friend picking and eating them when you were growing up.

"Those two girls were always so tight," I say to your friend's mother-auntie. "One couldn't eat a whole naseberry without offering half to the other one. It's true, right?"

"Hmm mmm," she says and looks down at her hands, clasped on her lap.

"I haven't been a good mother," I tell her. "I could have stood up for her and told her father that if he put her out I would leave, too. Why didn't I do that?"

"Nobody can think of everything," your friend's mother-auntie says.

"I gave her money, you know. I tried to make sure she didn't need anything. And people bought her paintings up there at the university when she stayed with your daughter."

"My niece. Cheryl," she corrects me, stressing the name. "Or maybe she is really my daughter." Then she laughs, a dry cackle like a granny.

I look at her face, Sweetheart, and I wonder how old she is. I know she can't be much older than me, but I feel that she has been around forever. She was already living here when we moved into this neighbourhood, and over the years I've always felt she was slightly off her rocker. But she is just a woman who doesn't like to talk, who keeps her words inside her head. I know she listens to everything I say, though, and I know she is brighter than people think. She, too, is probably an expert at stitching together a good raincoat so the water doesn't seep in.

That's the one thing I was good at in school, you know – home economics. Sewing and cooking. Not things that made my father jump for joy. We did embroidery on bits of calico cloth and I can still see the smile on that teacher's face – Miss Clary, I think – when she held up my work to the class. No one could embroider a red hibiscus flower like I could and make it look so real, with stems and leaves in green.

One term, Miss Clary-or-whoever decided that we would make raincoats, with hoods and all, in preparation for the rainy season. She brought in rolls of plastic and showed us how to cut a pattern, how to sew and then glue the sides together. And yes, mine was a work of art. When the coat was finished, we had to sponge water on the outside and see if the coat got wet on the inside, but mine was as dry as the skin on my elbow. Not a drop of moisture showed. I wore that raincoat for many years and, if I search the house today, I'm sure I'll find a remnant of the plastic somewhere.

Your father thinks I'm a fool, Sweetheart, but I know things, I feel things. And although I forget a lot, I remember a lot. As I said, don't bother me with dates and names, but once I see something, it stays with me. I can still picture your friend's mother-auntie's face at that wedding, when your friend's father married the rich woman on the hill. I saw her looking at the happy bride and groom, and I knew that if she could have poisoned them and got away with it, she would have.

I wonder if I have the same sign on my face now when I look at your father.

I have so many pictures in my brain of you growing up, of

you and your friend chatting in the house, playing on the piano. I remember your carrying that fluffy beige puppy down the road to her as a present. What did they name it, again? Salt or Scallion or something like that. A strange name for any animal. And that puppy grew into a lovely dog and lived a long-long time. Some people round here claim that the dog could see the future and would always howl when somebody was going to die. But it was your friend's mother-auntie who howled when the dog itself died. She came out one morning and saw it lying stiff on her verandah, and she let out a wail that echoed round everybody's yard. It turned my blood to ice when I heard it; I never knew anybody could feel that way about a dog.

Yes, I remember a lot, Sweetheart, too much probably. And sometimes I wonder if I am imagining things or if they really happened. Because, you know, I am not a bright woman.

Your father, now, he could've been a schoolteacher. He is a books man, a dates and numbers man. He, like my Papa, is one of the brightest people on this planet. You wouldn't believe that his own father could not read and write, would you? Didn't know A from B, or his left hand from his right. And yet your father can't stand ignorant people, as he loves to say.

That is his problem, poor thing. He wanted you and your brothers to be bright, and you all were determined not to be, almost as if to spite him. But he blamed me – a foolish woman who couldn't help but have fool-fool pickney. He could never see the things you were good at, yet I saw him bawling like a baby after the postman delivered your painting. I had to leave the house before I said words I would regret or asked questions without answers.

Would he have answered me, Sweetheart, if I asked why he sometimes went to your room late in the night when you were growing up? Why he stood there in the doorway, watching you sleep? I know in my heart that he never touched you, never hurt you, because you would have told me. I got up a couple of times and saw him there, standing like a ghost in the darkness.

"You'll frighten her if she wakes up and sees you," I told him.

"I'm just making sure she's all right," he answered. "I won't wake her up."

So many times I wanted to ask you, Sweetheart, if you knew he was there, but I never did, and now the moment is long past for questions. I only know that the painting you sent him means that you've forgiven him for everything.

"Do you think she has forgiven me?" I ask your friend's mother-auntie.

"Who, Dulcinea?"

"Yes, Dulcinea, my daughter."

She stares at her dogs for a long time without answering, then her head slowly bobs up and down.

CHAPTER ELEVEN

CHERYL

Kingston

Trevor is there to pick me up at the airport when I arrive back in Kingston. After being with Danny, I'm struck by how tightly Trev holds himself, how tense his facial muscles seem. Did you ever notice that about him, Dulci? He looks as if he expects the worst to happen and is prepared for it. Today I feel the same.

As always, it both pains and pleases us to see each other. We hug, and I hold onto him for longer than I've ever done. When we jerkily move apart, I notice that his red-rimmed brown eyes mirror my own.

He turns away to take my bag from the khaki-clad porter who has been standing silently watching us. I give the man the last of my American dollars, and he flashes me a wide smile at the unexpected amount. His pleasure normally would have cheered me up, Dulci, but right now I don't know how to shed this heaviness that's pushing me down.

"How was the trip?" Trev asks in his husky voice. It's one of the things I like most about him – this deep tone that suddenly materialized when he'd just turned fourteen. I remember both you and I teasing him, saying he should try to sing like Barry White. *Let the Music Play*. We use to mimic the soul man all the time, giggling. He was one of your mother's favourite singers and I think she used to play his records to annoy your father, who couldn't stand that bedroom voice.

I sigh in response to Trev's question. I feel drained and slightly disoriented, thrown by the blinding brightness of the sun. The island feels like an over-lit stage set, complete with blue mountains in the background, and Trev and I uneasy characters rehearsing our lines.

"It was okay. I did what Dulci wanted."

"I still can't believe she's gone."

I think *she isn't*, but I don't say it out loud because Trev would never understand how much you're with me, Dulci. When will I be able to let you go?

Trev shows me to the car in the parking lot and, as we open the doors, the hot air from within blasts our faces like the heat from an oven.

"Sorry," he says, grimacing. "There wasn't one tree left to park under."

"Don't worry. A little heat won't hurt us. There are worse things."

"Yeah. I know."

We smile at each other uncertainly, knowing there are secrets to impart but not sure where to begin.

"You first," I say, when we're on the Palisadoes with the sea stretching to our left, and the mountains in front of us like a challenge. I stare out the window at the children swimming at Gunboat Beach, so uncaring of the sun beating down on their backs. Tomorrow both they and I will be back in a classroom but I'm probably looking forward to it a lot more than they are.

"Me first what?" Trev asks with a slight laugh.

"You have something to tell me. What has my lovely aunt, your lovely mother been up to while I was in New York?"

He remains silent for a long while, eyes focused on the road, and just when I think he's not going to answer, he says with forced calmness: "We're not cousins."

Several interpretations of that rush through my mind: Aunt Mavis is not really my mother's sister, Trev is adopted, or he's met someone and is trying to dissociate himself from me.

"I mean," he clears his throat. "We're cousins as well as…" He can't seem to get the words out.

The truth dawns on me then, and I can hear you saying to me once more, Dulci: "The two of you look so much alike."

I start laughing, and the joyless sound fills the car until I manage to clamp my jaws together.

"Same father?" I ask finally.

"That's right," Trev confirms as if discussing some mundane item of news.

"Aunt Mavis told you?"

"Yeah, I got the whole story, from A to Z."

"Jesus! And Daddy knows?"

Trev doesn't respond, so I answer my own question. "Of course, he must've known all along. What a shit."

I put my hands over my face, trying to hold back I don't know what – screams, tears, rage. I want to ask Trev to stop the car so I can step outside to throw up, but instead I force the bile back down.

"I'm sorry," I croak, unable to control my voice.

"Nothing to be sorry about," Trev says without looking at me. He takes his hand off the gear-stick and holds mine for a few seconds. "You think it would've made a difference if we'd known?"

"Yes. Maybe. I don't know. But they should've told us. I hate them."

"That's not going to help."

I kiss my teeth. When did Trev get so blasted wise, Dulci?

"So, what now?" I ask.

"This doesn't change anything for me. We have our own lives to live."

"You're crazy, Trev. It changes everything. We can't just carry on as if…"

His face becomes more taut as some kind of stubbornness sets in. "As I said, it doesn't change anything for me. That man is not my father. Never has been."

I reach across and put my hand on the back of his neck, gently massaging the rigid tendons, feeling the soft curls at his hairline. We've touched each other in so many different ways, but I've never touched him like this – like a sister, trying to give comfort.

As we leave the coast behind, I finally close my eyes and lean my head against the headrest, trying to still the hammering at my temples.

"You had something to tell me too. Was it about Dulci? What did she really die from?" Trev's voice seems to come from across the sea.

"Cancer," I reply. "And she said she was ready to go."

"She was always something else. I know how much you're going to miss her. No more trips to New York every holiday."

I can see you chuckling, Dulci, and I know that now is the time I should tell Trev about Danny. But I can't bring myself to. Later. For sure. After a word with Auntie Mavis. And my rass-claat father.

CHAPTER TWELVE

CHERYL

Kingston: The Cinea Verse Retrospective

Well, Dulci, after making a lot of noise for a year, the Tourist Board did get the retrospective ready in time for your first "anniversary". And what a whole heap of excitement. My dear, you would have loved it. Trev and I, Aunt Mavis, your mother and father, your five brothers, and everybody else and his dog all descended on the National Gallery at Ocean Boulevard. One of the first guests to arrive was Carlton Beckett, who turned up with his wife. Yes, Machete-Lady Dakota herself, dressed like she was going to King's House, in a long maroon-coloured velvety dress. I hadn't a clue what to say when Carlton introduced us, so I just grinned like an idiot, and she smiled back. She actually seemed like a nice person, imagine that! I wondered why she was still with Carlton. Do you think he explained the connection between you and me?

His bank donated loads of money to help sponsor the event (he must still have a guilty conscience), but the Tourist Board people were the ones who took charge of all the organizing. They really do know how to spice things up, how to bring in the crowds with live music and free drinks and food. I don't think the National Gallery had ever seen such a bacchanal, though lately they'd been emphasizing that they wanted to bring art to a wider audience and to involve the "residents of the downtown area". I guess that's why they hired current dancehall delight, Meanie Man. He started things off with a song he'd written especially for you, "Girl, You're Home", where art rhymed with fart, and painting rhymed with dating. I could see that some people didn't know whether to laugh or leave, but his eight minutes on the stage mercifully passed, and we had the Jamrock Military Band playing "By the Rivers of Babylon" and "I Can See Clearly Now". I told the conductor that you'd liked "No Woman No Cry", and the band played that as well, before ending up with "Oh Carolina". Even Aunt Mavis was swaying.

The Tourist Board had given away quite a few airline tickets and so managed to attract a bunch of foreign journalists – who presumably all promised to write glowing articles about the island. No matter what we do, we must never forget we are a tourist destination.

Josh Scarbinsky led the pack of renowned international art experts. I had recommended that he do the catalogue, and the Tourist Board dutifully paid him a bagful of money. He's now *the* authority on this region, you know. His book came out just last month – *From Voodoo to Verse: The Magic of Caribbean Art*. I haven't read it, but it's on my list of things to buy. Perhaps he'll offer me a free copy? Anyway, he gave a lovely speech about your work, full of words such as "paradigmatic", "decolonization", "transculturation", "socio-political" and "intuitive".

"Of all the people present in this gallery, I probably knew Cinea best because she was my wife," he proclaimed. "So it's an honour for me to be here, among her family, friends and admirers, in her homeland." We all clapped politely, but not before Aunt Mavis had given off a rude snort of laughter and muttered: "Is who him talking bout, I wonder?" The woman just cannot behave herself, no matter where she is. At least tonight she had listened to me and was dressed decently, in a bright green frock, which made her look so much younger. I had also done her hair and put a bit of make-up on her face, with her complaining the whole time I was doing it: "I don't care what I look like or what people want to say about me, so why you goin' to all this trouble?" But when she looked in the mirror, I could see that she was pleased with the result.

You know, I've always thought of her as ancient but she is not even an old woman yet, not really. The painting you gave her as a thank-you for the anointment all those years ago is part of the three-month-long retrospective, as are the ones you left in my dorm room. The government wants to buy them from us but we've refused to sell. And I'll never part with the sketches you did, those last days in New York. Besides, I have enough money from the sale of the works at Gaucho Gallery. In the letter you left behind, you said that the money was to help me stay out of the classroom.

And I've thought about resigning, Dulci, but a funny thing is that I finally realize how much I like teaching. What else would I do?

My father and Gloria Armstrong were there, too, at the National Gallery. Gloria's teeth are protruding more than ever these days; she really needs to get them fixed before they cause someone irreparable damage. And my father looked like a younger version of Morgan Freeman, decked out in a white shirt and bow tie. Aunt Mavis ignored both of them the whole afternoon. I still don't know if Daddy realizes that Trev and I now know the truth. I couldn't bring myself to talk to him about it. And it doesn't matter much anyway because we long ago stopped waiting for him to come back.

After Josh gave his speech, Gloria came to tell me excitedly that she'd managed to acquire two paintings that you'd done when you must have been about eighteen or nineteen. A security guard whom she'd successfully defended against murder charges had given them to her, she said.

"He told me that Dulci brought him the paintings as a present after he saved her from being chopped up by some madwoman. Do you know anything about that, Cheryl?" Gloria asked, staring at me in her lawyer-fashion. I would have to tell the truth, wouldn't I?

"Not a thing," I replied. "I would get them checked out by an expert if I were you."

Gloria looked so terribly disappointed that I had to bite my lip to stop myself from laughing. I hadn't a clue that she liked art, but I guess she has walls to fill, and that mansion must get lonely sometimes with just her, my father and the live-in helper there.

Still, everybody now wants to lay hands on those early pieces that you signed "Dulci", before you became Cinea. You must find it all so amusing.

The Minister of Education, Youth and Culture took to the podium next, as expected. Good old Shabba Cranky. You must remember him – he had a few dancehall hits when we were in our teens. Well, he got chosen in the elections a few months ago, amidst much hue and cry about whether he can even read and write. People can be so biased, right? Just because the guy has gold teeth and likes to wear gold chains, they think he's a fool. Believe me, I've learned my lesson, and when I listen to his rap lyrics I know that I'm hearing superior intelligence. You liked him, too.

"As a sovereign nation, we've produced many notable sons and daughters – musicians, dancers, sportsmen and sportswomen, writers and artists," Shabba recited, not even looking at the paper in his hand. "But Cinea Verse was among the best. She brought international renown to our small part of the world, just like Bob Marley and yours truly did before her. She was and will remain a shining example to our youth of what can be achieved with hard work and willpower."

"And don't forget a little obeah and a trip to America," I whispered to Trev, who rolled his eyes. I wish my half-brother, cousin, whatever, had a better sense of humour. But both he and I are emotional mules, aren't we? Dependable, reliable, protective, yes; but still something gone wrong in the crossbreeding.

Danny, now, he loves a good joke, just like you. From the moment I met him on the plane, when I was taking bits of you back to New York, he made me laugh. And I need laughter more than anything else right now. I miss him when he goes to New York, and although he wants me to travel with him, I can't go there anymore.

Trev is still brooding about our separation, but we all know it's for the best. How long could we have continued like that? Years of tiptoeing eventually take their toll, and even Aunt Mavis had started remarking on how skinny I was getting. My mathematician's brain of neatly dividing and sectoring can take only so much. Trev has been talking about giving up his job and going to live in the hills for a while, "to think about things". Aunt Mavis has a house in The Cockpit Country, left to her by our great-grandmother, and she told Trevor he could live there if he wanted. I'm worried about his being up there by himself, but Aunt Mavis says he'll be fine, as if she knows him better than I do. She says that maybe he can help the people up there, now that mining companies want to go in and tear up the land, looking for bauxite. I really can't see Trev tying himself to a tree to prevent it being chopped down or standing in the path of a tractor. But maybe he'll surprise us all.

Shabba's speech was getting way too long, as he recited a

never-ending list of the "government's stupendous achievements" in the field of culture; so I decided to go for a walk. We both loved this part of Kingston, Dulci. You used to drag me here every other month to look at an exhibition. But once we were in the gallery, you would rapidly go from painting to painting as if you couldn't wait to get out, while I would linger, examining every variation in colour. We both liked to look at Gonzales' sculpture of Bob Marley, which had been banished to the gallery instead of being erected in a public place because people had hated it so much. The pose was that of a rebel, and it really was much better than the tame statue that replaced it.

I wandered along Ocean Boulevard, looking at the sea, my dress whipping about me in the breeze. I stopped at the Cruise Ship Pier, thinking of the tourists we used to see nervously disembarking once upon a time, before riots and pickpockets chased them back to the safety of the north coast. Across the water I could see the long strip of the Palisadoes, and I watched as a plane came in to land at the airport. A few months ago, floods shut everything down and travellers had to make the trip to Montego Bay instead. Now the government wants to move the airport inland to shield it from hurricanes. But I don't think people will ever get used to *not* seeing the sea and the Blue Mountains in the background as they return home from abroad. Not that any of it matters to me; I won't be doing much flying any more.

The narrow finger of the Palisadoes ends in Port Royal, where we went so many times. The wickedest city on earth. But it's famous now for Babsy's Fish Restaurant, where people go on weekends for fried fresh fish, the best bammy anywhere, and a shot of rum. You were already in New York when Babsy (actually a Chinese man) started the business, so you never joined Trev and me there.

The breeze on Ocean Boulevard made my throat dry, so I bought a coconut from one of the vendors along the waterfront and drank thirstily through a straw, the liquid filling me, the taste sending me back years, to that week when I had dengue fever at university. You fed me coconut-water then because Aunt Mavis had told you over the phone that it would cool me on the inside, while the wet washcloth would bring the fever down on the outside. You sent Trev to fetch the coconuts at Papine market, and you propped pillows behind my back and held the straw to my lips, urging me to drink.

The fever was stubborn, though. As soon as I had a moment of clarity and smiled at feeling better, it would come back higher than before. It brought strange shadowy dreams, of Aunt Mavis and my father arguing in furious hushed tones, and looking surprised when they saw me watching them; of you calling my name over and over from a long distance away; of a hand in my hair, gently massaging my scalp. I remember babbling and getting agitated when I woke up once to find someone kissing the corner of my lips and caressing my face. I thought it was Trev, who had been in the room earlier, bickering with you that I needed to go to the hospital, which was right there on campus. My head pounded with urgent questions, but the fever sent me somewhere else. And the caresses came again and again, like a feather being brushed against my overheated skin.

"It wasn't Trev," you told me finally in New York, and that's when I broke down. I accused you of being selfish, for never telling me, for wanting to go.

"What would you have done if you'd known?" you asked. "Would we have stayed friends?" But that was a question with no answer.

If I had known, would Cinea Verse have been born? Would Dulci Evers be there now, standing at the waterfront with me, laughing in the afternoon breeze sweeping over Ocean Boulevard? What a view, you might have said, as the sun cast its saffron light on the sea, creating a perfect

Caribbean postcard-scene. I was the one who'd been self-ish, Dulci, for wanting to hold on, for begging you to stay when you'd made up your mind to go. You didn't want to be a "survivor", and that was your choice to make. Aunt Mavis, Trev and I – we're survivors, but there is nothing heroic in putting one foot in front of the other just to keep going on a meaningless path. When I talked about you with Aunt Mavis – telling her, as I've told everyone, that you wanted to go – she gave a dry laugh.

"Dulcinea lucky she can make that kind of decision," she said. "When *I* wanted to go, I had you and Trevor to think 'bout."

That made me see her in a new light, Dulci. Imagine, Trev and I kept her alive, even though we couldn't get her to talk until now.

I retraced my steps to the National Gallery, hoping that Shabba was almost done. When I entered the hall, he was making the announcement that everyone had been waiting for. You were to get a medal, Dulci: the Order of Merit, for your "international eminence" in the field of the arts. Shabba called up the Governor General to make the presentation, and your father went up to accept it. He was crying like a baby.

"My daughter was… my daughter was…" he blubbered into the microphone. But we never found out what you were, Dulci, because he finally just said "thank you" and walked off the platform, back to your mother's side. She smiled at him as he gave her the medal. She looked so regal that I couldn't help staring.

The Tourist Board had asked me to speak as well, but what was I going to say? You already knew everything, Dulcinea Gertrude Evers.

All Peepal Tree titles are available from the website
www.peepaltreepress.com
with a money back guarantee, secure credit card
ordering
and fast delivery throughout the world at cost or less.

E-mail: contact@peepaltreepress.com

ALSO BY ALECIA MCKENZIE

Stories from Yard
ISBN: 9781900715621; pp. 180; pub. 2005; £7.99

Fear and bitterness pollute the ground from which the characters of these stories, mostly young and female, struggle to grow. With so many 'bad seeds', mostly male, taking root around them, with sexual violence, neglectful and brutal fathers, jealousy, lies and prejudice obscuring their light, their blossoming is always under threat. But in these diverse, subtly constructed stories, there is often a glimmer of hope: in a girl's tentative resistance to the general prejudice about 'madmen'; or in the silence on a phone line between estranged friends, where forgiveness may or may not come.

In the stories set in Jamaica life is hard, and the comforts of 'away' are idealized. But in the cold of the streets of the North, there is no passport to success for the people of yard. Only their resilience, optimism, humour and friendship (and the comforts of beer and ganja) help them make their way. And in the 'diaspora dance' of the different immigrant nations struggling to find their place in Europe or North America, new connections and new possibilities are being created.

But if these stories are coolly unsentimental, there is also room for humour and moments of joy, as when Marie, a middle-aged Jamaican reggae singer, finds the sweet flavour of cane juice lingering on her young Brazilian lover's tongue.

ABOUT THE AUTHOR

Alecia McKenzie was born in Kingston, Jamaica. She started writing while at high school, and her poems were published in local newspapers *The Gleaner* and *The Star*. Her first collection of short stories, *Satellite City*, won the regional Commonwealth Writers Prize for Best First Book. Her other books include *Stories from Yard*, *Doctor's Orders* and *When the Rain Stopped in Natland*. Her work has also appeared in literary magazines and various anthologies such as *Stories from Blue Latitudes*, *Global Tales* and the first *Girls' Night In*.

Besides Jamaica, Alecia has lived in the United States, Belgium, the UK, Singapore and France, where she has pursued her love of literature, art and journalism. She and her family return as often as possible to the Caribbean.